Shakespeare's Apprentice

Veronica Bennett worked for several years as an English lecturer but now devotes her time to writing fiction. She is the author of *Angelmonster*, *The Boy-free Zone*, *Cassandra's Sister*, *Fish Feet*, *Monkey* and, for younger readers, *Dandelion and Bobcat*. On writing *Shakespeare's Apprentice* Veronica says, "Not surprisingly, this story was inspired by Shakespeare. The fact that in Elizabethan theatre women were played by teenage boys has always intrigued me. The lives of these apprentice players must have been astonishingly busy. They and other actors had to take on several roles in the same play. Companies would do ten or more performances a week, of three or four different plays, with the public demanding a new play about every six weeks. I began to wonder how it felt to work at this relentless pace, performing daily before a rowdy, unforgiving crowd. And what would happen if an apprentice stepped out of line in that violent, suspicious world, daring to do something not even a character in a Shakespeare play would risk..." Veronica is married to a university professor and has two children.

SHAKESPEARE'S APPRENTICE

Veronica Bennett

WALKER BOOKS

This is a work of fiction. Names, characters, places and incidents are
either the product of the author's imagination or, if real, are used fictitiously.

First published 2007 by Walker Books Ltd
87 Vauxhall Walk, London SE11 5HJ

2 4 6 8 10 9 7 5 3 1

Text © 2007 Veronica Bennett
Cover illustration © 2007 David Holmes

This book has been typeset in M Bembo and Stuyvesant ICG

Printed by Creative Print and Design, Wales

British Library Cataloguing in Publication Data:
a catalogue record for this book
is available from the British Library

ISBN 978-1-84428-148-0

www.walkerbooks.co.uk

For my editor, Mara Bergman

Dramatis Personae

MEMBERS OF THE LORD CHAMBERLAIN'S MEN:

Sam Gilburne
William Hughes
Robert Goughe
Nathan Field

Apprentice actors

William Shakespeare

Playwright, actor and
sharer (part owner)

Richard Burbage
John Heminges
Augustine Phillips
Thomas Pope
William Kempe
Robert Armin

Actors (sharers and hired men)

Cuthbert Burbage

Non-actor, sharer and brother
to Richard Burbage

NOT OF THE COMPANY:

Robert Devereux, 2nd Earl of Essex
Henry Wriothesley, 3rd Earl of Southampton
Lords and Knights of the Essex–Southampton circle

Queen Elizabeth I

Lady Lucie Cheetham	Niece to Lord Essex
Lady Penelope Rich	Sister to Lord Essex
Lady Frances Essex	Wife to Lord Essex
Matty	Servant to Lady Lucie
Clarice Gilburne	Sister to Sam Gilburne

Citizens of London, lords and ladies, relatives and friends
of the company.

THE ACTION OF THE STORY TAKES PLACE FROM LATE 1598
TO EARLY 1601.

The Company

"One line! One line in the entire scene! I tell you, William, I am heartsick of playing such small parts."

"Then you must grow a few inches," said William Hughes. He flicked the pages of the script. "See here, the lady Hero is described as 'short' because *you* always play her."

"Very diverting," said Sam, lunging for the script.

William held it out of his reach. "How now, little one, what ails you?" he cried in his high-pitched stage voice. "Jealous, are you?"

It was futile to fight with William, and Sam did not wish to anyway. He sat down dejectedly on the dusty stage.

William relented. "There. Look at it if you must, though you surely know it by heart." He threw the script at Sam's feet. "And be of good cheer, for Hero has some fine poetry later in the play."

Sam and William had both acted in *Much Ado About Nothing* many times. So many, indeed, that they knew each other's lines as well as their own. "True, the lady Hero speaks poetry," Sam agreed, "but the part of the lady Beatrice is a hundred times larger. You are hardly off the stage."

Sam *was* jealous. Beatrice had witty lines that set the house roaring, and plenty of clowning to do, which Mr Shakespeare said Sam had a gift for. Yet this coveted leading part had again gone to William, who, for all his swaggering, was only a year and a half older than Sam. The truth was, William Hughes was a favourite of Mr Shakespeare. Sam knew it, Mr Shakespeare knew it, everyone knew it. And as everyone also knew, what Mr Shakespeare chose to do was not questioned by apprentices like Sam.

"But at least in this play I cannot be called upon to double," he continued. "I will not be changing my costume fifty times, and forgetting what I am to say, and sweating like a serving wench."

William sat down on the throne left at the back of the stage after yesterday's performance of *A Midsummer Night's Dream*. The theatre known as the "Curtain" was empty. Earlier it had witnessed the raucous spectacle of cockfighting, but the next performance of the *Dream* would not be presented until the following afternoon. "Apart from the obvious one," he observed, "there is no difference between an apprentice and a serving wench. Be reasonable, Sam. The only reason I get larger parts is that I have been an apprentice longer than you."

"My thanks for those comforting words."

William looked down at Sam, half closing his eyes and drawing his hand across his forehead as Sam had seen older actors do. "Now, all this talk of serving wenches is affecting my concentration. And I have, as you so obligingly point out, a vast number of lines to revise. Pray, leave me to my labours."

Sam was not in a humour to be amused. He knew that William was a true friend who would defend him and the other Lord Chamberlain's Men to the death. But today a cloud had settled on Sam, showering him with resentment. He lay down on his back, stretching his legs and arms, and looked at the circle of white December sky framed by the rafters of the building.

This was the life Sam had chosen. These boys and men were his friends as well as his masters and fellow apprentices. He even shared lodgings with William and another apprentice, Robert Goughe; they were his family now. Shoreditch, with its two theatres, where crowds came every afternoon to the play, or the bears, or the dogs, or to see juggling, or dancing, or to dance themselves, was a familiar world within the wider world of London. He had chosen it as his workplace and his home.

But how long must a boy wait to play a part like Beatrice? Sam was sixteen; he could no longer play children or, as had lately been so publicly proven, Juliet. *Romeo and Juliet*, a favourite play, had provided Sam for the last three years with a leading part. But, upon its most recent revival, Mr Shakespeare had demoted Sam to playing Juliet's mother and doubling as a female courtier, a torchbearer and a nameless "friend" of Romeo. The part of Juliet had been given to thirteen-year-old, pure-voiced, smooth-skinned Nathan Field.

"'Asleep, my love? What, dead, my dove?'"

A boot was kicking Sam's side gently. It belonged to Mr Augustine Phillips, who, as a senior actor and a sharer in the company, could be as sarcastic as he liked towards an apprentice and expect no retort.

"Accurately quoted and excellently delivered, sir," was the most Sam could dare. "But I was neither asleep nor dead. I was, as your choice of quotation from *A Midsummer Night's Dream* might suggest, dreaming."

"Of what, might I ask?"

Mr Phillips seemed amused as he watched Sam get to his feet. Hat brushed and carefully placed, script in one hand, while the other rested upon the hilt of his sword, he stood in an apparently languid but actually alert pose, every inch the actor, every inch the gentleman. One day, thought Sam, one day…

"Of acting. What else is there, sir?" he said respectfully.

"What else indeed?" agreed Mr Phillips. "Are you to be my Beatrice?"

Sam knew that the senior man knew perfectly well he was not. But apprentices were expected to make sport for their employers. Any sign of discomfiture shown by Sam would hand Mr Phillips the point, and Sam was determined not to give it to him.

"I cannot be," he said, his gaze resting on Mr Phillips's face as he made the older man a small bow. "With respect, sir, if you would but read the first scene, you will see that Hero, your lady's cousin, is written down by Mr Shakespeare as 'brown' and 'little'. As your own eyes tell you, I am short of stature and brown of hair. I am cast before the pen has left the page."

Mr Phillips laughed. "So you are! And which of your

fellows has Mr Shakespeare decided shall be my lady, then? Ah!" He turned, deliberately slowly, to behold William, who was still sitting on the throne, smiling graciously. "The beautiful Mr Hughes!"

William *was* beautiful, there was no denying. Not only a head taller than Sam, but fine-boned in a way that Nature had decreed Sam could never be, and possessed of eyes so blue and hair so strikingly golden that William's loyal followers, both men and women, came again and again to the theatre for the spectacle of an exquisitely made boy wearing the head-dress, corset and skirt of an exquisitely made girl.

As Sam well knew, parts for William would only increase in stature as he grew older. He would play noblemen and kings – no, perhaps kings would have to wait until the great Mr Richard Burbage retired – and another apprentice, as yet unknown, would take on the mantle of Beatrice. And Sam? Sam would go on being "short" Hero until his voice was too low and his beard too obvious, when he would be trusted with the part of the lead actor's friend, enemy, brother or cousin.

Or perhaps his horse, he thought discontentedly, watching Augustine Phillips take William's hand and kiss it. He looked the other way. That kind of dalliance was expected in the theatre, but it did not mean Sam wanted it for himself. Let William fascinate old men and be pleased with himself. Sam himself was much more interested in fascinating young women, if only he could meet some.

From behind the stage came raised voices. "Not on until halfway through! Then, pray, why am I here? Do you not know, Master Shakespeare, that I am an important man with important concerns? I have drinking and drabbing to do!"

"Mr Kempe, your importance lies not in drinking and drabbing – anyone can do that," came Mr Shakespeare's voice, resigned but tolerant. "But who will show these lily-livered lads how to raise a laugh from *Much Ado About Nothing* if you will not? Now, make haste. We must begin or the daylight will be gone before you make your first entrance."

"The daylight will be gone before we are done with a quarter of the play," grumbled Mr Kempe. "And I cannot make haste, Will, with my old legs."

"Shall we save your old legs, then, by abandoning the dance at the end of the play?" asked Mr Shakespeare, appearing at the back of the stage. "It is no trouble to change the lines."

"No, no, sir, do not do that! For what is a comedy without dancing?"

Mr Kempe, who had been the company clown for more years than any of the apprentices knew, followed Mr Shakespeare, his hat on the back of his head and his great round face shining with the effects of a visit to a tavern.

"A comedy without dancing would be a worthless production that would never be performed by the Lord Chamberlain's Men," volunteered William Hughes. "And certainly not by Mr William Kempe, whose dancing is justly famed throughout England."

The two Williams bowed to each other. Contempt for his friend's flattery, freely despatched even when there was no hope of reward, rushed over Sam so suddenly he hardly knew how to hide it. Mr Shakespeare came to Sam's side and spoke in a low voice. "A pretty pair, do you not agree?"

Sam bowed, but could not very well reply.

"Our profession is crowded with coxcombs, knaves and mindless slaves, is it not, Master Gilburne?"

"I know not what you mean, sir," said Sam guardedly.

"I think you do," replied his master.

"Leave the lad alone, Will," said John Heminges. He and Robert Armin, who was to play and sing the music in *Much Ado About Nothing*, had entered the theatre by the main door.

Mr Shakespeare turned to the new arrivals. "Ah, John. You were ever a champion of the apprentices."

"And rightly so." Mr Heminges mounted the stage. "Do not underestimate a boy," he advised Mr Shakespeare. "Sam Gilburne may surprise us yet."

Sam coloured, was ashamed, and coloured more deeply.

"Observe," said Mr Heminges, "this boy is neatly dressed, humble, polite and punctual, which cannot be said of all our apprentices, as I hardly need tell you. Master Robert Goughe is doubtless lying abed still, like the simpleton he is, and that milksop Nathan Field would rather hold his mother's apron-strings than attend to his employment."

Out of the corner of his eye Sam saw the curtain at the back of the stage twitch. Tom Pope put his head around it and grimaced at the rest of the assembly. "Too cold for a rehearsal," he complained. "Far, far too cold.

Let us to Mistress Turville's, and forget all about it."

"Mr Pope, for all that you are a young man, you are an old woman," said Mr Phillips. "Get yourself a cloak from the costume store if your mother has not wrapped you in warm enough swaddling-clothes today, and stop your talk of Mistress Turville's. You will get a drink there soon enough, when your work is finished."

Tom Pope did not argue. He was a sharer in the company as well as a hired man, but very newly appointed. Mr Phillips was his senior in both age and position. "Tom Pope needs a wench to keep him warm," observed Mr Phillips, smiling. "Come, Sam Gilburne, will you not wrap him in your skirt?"

"Nay, Augustine," contradicted Mr Heminges. "Do not redden the ears of the poor boy any further. Sam's inclinations do not that way lie. Better ask William Hughes."

"Nothing will redden the ears of any of our apprentices, Mr Heminges," said Mr Armin. "After a few years in our company they are immune to lewdness of any description. Is that not so, Master Hughes?"

William, who never minded this sort of banter, sat serenely upon his throne, regarding the company from narrowed eyes. "I can supply a wench's skirt," he said, "but not what hides beneath it. Mr Pope may well be disappointed."

During the laughter that this caused, Sam sighed to himself. If William were a real girl Sam would not mind his ever-present flirtatiousness. But looking like a girl and acting girls' parts was not the same as actually being a girl. Why did the older men in the company never tire of alluding to this, and William never tire of responding?

"Now, gentlemen," said Mr Shakespeare as the laughter dispersed. "May I remind you that we are here to rehearse a play, for the performance of which we have already been paid? Here are your parts." He pointed to each player as he said their character's name, then finally ended with, "I will take the part of the messenger, and the only other part in the first scene is to be played by … let me see … no, that is all."

"Pardon me, Mr Shakespeare," ventured Sam, feeling foolish.

"What is it, boy?"

"I am in this scene. I am the lady Hero."

Mr Shakespeare consulted the script, his large eyes squinting to see it better.

"I have one line, sir," prompted Sam. "It is after one of Mr Pope's lines. Just here." He pointed.

"I see," said Mr Shakespeare, nodding. "There is your line, indeed," he said solemnly. "You had better not forget it, had you, Master Sam?"

"I shall not, sir."

"Get you within, then."

Sam joined Mr Pope inside the curtained space at the back of the stage, and the rehearsal began. As he did not have much to do, Sam entertained himself in his usual way, by watching Mr Phillips. Augustine Phillips had played the part of Benedick, Beatrice's lover in *Much Ado About Nothing*, as many times as William had played Beatrice. But Mr Shakespeare had decided that he was not satisfied with their first exchange, and had ordered more rehearsal.

William Hughes and Mr Phillips did the exchange twice, then a third time. Sam observed Mr Phillips's skill in speaking and pausing, allowing for laughter, impressing his observers not only with his voice but with his whole form. He turned, he gestured, he worked his features hard enough for those at the back of the highest gallery to see his expressions. He was so accomplished it was as if he did it by magic.

In the three years since Sam had embarked on his apprenticeship he had become accustomed to the unrelenting nature of a player's life. The Lord Chamberlain's Men performed several different plays every week, so Sam had to learn and rehearse his lines very quickly, often without even seeing a complete script. During a first performance he was sometimes as curious about the ending of the play as the audience. But he had soon discovered that it was this very uncertainty that gave the company a camaraderie impossible to imagine in other professions. Never quite knowing exactly how anything would turn out, although frightening, was definitely exciting.

Sam could not count the months since he had last seen his mother and father. How tall would his brothers be by now? And was his sister Clarice really a young lady of fourteen? Time seemed governed more rigidly by the activity of the playhouse than any calendar. But God and hard work willing, Sam and his friends Robert and William – he could not yet countenance the notion of calling that upstart Nathan his friend – would eventually attain the stature of Mr Phillips and Mr Kempe, or even Mr Burbage. To be a tragic actor like

Richard Burbage was the greatest prize in the theatrical profession. Sam could not remember what it was like not to tread this stage every day in the company of these men. It was his life, as it had always been theirs.

"Masters!" A shout arose from under the stage. The trapdoor opened and Nathan Field's untidy hair and lopsided cap appeared. "Masters, gentlemen all, listen to what I have to tell!"

"Whatever it is," observed Mr Phillips, "it had better excuse this unorthodox entrance. What do you mean, boy, by invading our peace like this?"

"It is the quickest way from the street, sir," explained Nathan. "Master Robert and I, we have been lately at The Theatre, and I have run from there as fast as I could."

"And where is Master Robert now?"

"Still there, sir. Will you hear my news?"

"If you have breath enough to utter it," said Mr Phillips, less haughtily. Nathan's mention of the nearby playhouse named "The Theatre" gave notice of news of a most interesting nature. "Speak, boy."

"We heard Mr Allen and Mr Burbage talking – Mr Richard Burbage's brother, that is, sir. Mr Cuthbert Burbage."

"We know of whom you speak, Master Nathan," said Mr Heminges. He and the other members of the company were gathered around the trapdoor. Every eye was on Nathan as he perched below them, glowing with importance.

"Robert and I were under the seats, sir, sharing a flagon of … getting by heart our parts for this rehearsal, sir."

"And you chose to do so in the presence of our sworn enemy, Mr Giles Allen, in The Theatre, a playhouse that is rightfully ours, but we cannot enter?" cried Mr Shakespeare. "You and that witless Robert Goughe are greater idiots even than I thought!"

"You will not scold me, sir, when I tell you what we heard," replied Nathan bravely. "Mr Cuthbert Burbage was saying that the Lord Chamberlain's Men shall soon be without a place to perform in, as we shall be turned out of the Curtain within the month. He asked him whether, as a Christian, he would consider extending the lease on The Theatre."

"And what did Mr Allen say?" asked Mr Phillips.

"He said he would never, in any circumstances under heaven, extend the lease. And he called Mr Burbage a rogue, sir."

"It is Allen that is the rogue!" cried Mr Kempe. "That grasping, whey-faced blockhead! I say we take back The Theatre by force!"

"Peace, Mr Kempe." Mr Shakespeare squatted beside the trapdoor, his eyes fixed upon Nathan's earnest face. "And what did Mr Burbage say then?"

"Mr Burbage said that if Mr Allen will not agree to extend the lease, then action will be taken to repossess the building, whether Mr Allen likes it or no," reported Nathan.

"'Action will be taken to repossess the building,'" repeated Mr Shakespeare. "If I am not mistaken, gentlemen, that is lawyers' talk. Cuthbert is using not only his own brains, but the services of the law to help him. What happened then, boy?"

Nathan's air of importance increased. "Mr Burbage told Mr Allen that if he, Mr Allen, chose not to read the terms of the lease with due and proper attention, he would live to rue his carelessness. Then, Mr Shakespeare, sir, he said Mr Allen might find he does not own The Theatre after all!"

There was a baffled silence. Every member of the Lord Chamberlain's Men knew that Mr Giles Allen owned The Theatre. Mr Allen was a businessman who could make more in one month from putting on bear-baiting, cockfighting, acrobats and dancers at the theatre than plays could earn for him in three. So when the lease had run out, Mr Allen had refused to renew it. The Lord Chamberlain's Men had lost their home.

The Theatre had stood empty for months while the quarrel raged. Meanwhile, the Lord Chamberlain's Men had been allowed by a kindlier landlord to perform temporarily at the nearby Curtain, the theatre in which they now stood. Mr Shakespeare had promised his players that somehow he would get them their own theatre back. He had even sworn to do it by the last day of the year. But now, as they rehearsed *Much Ado About Nothing* under this freezing December sky, the quarrel was still unresolved, and the landlord of the Curtain was becoming anxious for them to be gone.

"Indeed?" Mr Phillips was the first to speak. "And what did Mr Allen say in reply?"

"He called him a whoreson liar, sir."

"And did Mr Cuthbert Burbage defend himself against this charge?"

"Yes, sir, he said he spoke true, and Mr Allen called

him a worthless jackanapes whose tongue should be cut out."

"I am not surprised at Mr Allen's resorting to abuse," said Mr Shakespeare. He stood up and looked at the men, his face very serious. "He is as ignorant of whatever plan is in Cuthbert's head as we are. But he knows that there are many of us and one of him, and we are becoming impatient."

"I still say we fight him," declared Mr Kempe. "Desperate circumstances demand desperate resolutions. I may not be in constant practice, Master Shakespeare, but my sword is as sharp as the next man's."

"And so would mine be, if I had one," piped up William Hughes, "but I will defend the Lord Chamberlain's Men with my bare hands."

"Gentlemen," cut in Tom Pope, whom Sam had often seen outwit more loquacious men or settle disputes with a few words. "Bloodshed will not get us our theatre back. More likely, it will increase the Master of the Revels's conviction that we players are no better than a band of brigands. Mr Allen should fear danger of a more intellectual kind. We shall hear soon enough from Mr Cuthbert Burbage. Let us leave it to him and his brother to do what is best for the company."

Mr Phillips nodded. "Tom, for all your complaining you have the coolest head among us. If Mr Allen does indeed not own The Theatre after all, only good can come of it. But until Mr Cuthbert Burbage, or perhaps Master Goughe, who is still hiding under the seats at The Theatre, brings us further information, rejoicing will be premature." Twitching his cloak, he resumed his place on the stage. "Now, a long time ago, I believe we began the rehearsal of a play we are to put before the public tomorrow afternoon, and before Her Majesty at court the day after Christmas, which is barely a week hence. Field, shut that trapdoor, and let us continue."

"Though we have little light left, Augustine," said Mr Shakespeare, looking at the sky. "Tomorrow, gentlemen, is the shortest day of the year. I thank you, Master Nathan, for your intelligence. Now we have only to wonder what has befallen your bold companion, Master Robert Goughe."

"If Allen catches him, he'll skin him alive!" declared Mr Kempe, chuckling.

"Let us hope, with some fervour, that it does not come to that," said Mr Shakespeare.

Mr Heminges, Mr Pope, Mr Phillips and William continued the rehearsal. Sam, who had already spoken his one line and left the stage, sat on the straw-strewn floor of the yard and pondered on what he had heard.

It was typical of Nathan and Robert to do something as foolhardy as listen to Giles Allen's private conversation. But Sam envied them their foolhardiness, just as he envied William his good looks and easy self-advertisement. He knew that he did not want to amble, lisp or nickname God's creatures like a real girl in order to gain better roles. But, equally, he did not want always to be young Master Gilburne, always ready, always word perfect, always in the right place, and yet invisible. He wanted those who had influence over his future at least to *see* him.

"Sam! *Sam!*"

It was a whisper, just audible, coming from the lowest tier of the gallery. Without looking round, Sam edged nearer. "Robert?"

"Did Nathan tell Mr Shakespeare what happened at The Theatre?"

Robert's voice was muffled, as if there were something over his mouth. In the shadows, Sam could just make out the shape of his friend's cap. "Yes, he did. What is the matter, Robert?"

"What did Mr Shakespeare say?"

"He thinks Mr Burbage must have consulted a lawyer, and we may yet get The Theatre back. Look, why are you hiding? The rehearsal is almost over. You might as well come out."

"I cannot."

"Why?" asked Sam, forgetting to whisper.

"Shh! I do not want anyone else to know I am here."

"Why not?"

"You will know when you see me. Now, help me!"

Sam heard desperation in Robert's voice. "What would you ask?"

"That you come away, and meet me outside. Nobody will mark it, they are busy with the play."

Sam went to stand up, but Robert's next sharp whisper brought him down again. "And Sam, will you bring something from the costume store? Something like an old shirt or kerchief? It must not matter that it becomes stained." Sam heard him catch his breath. "It will be stained with my blood."

Enter Lady Lucie

$\mathcal{B}$y the time Sam and Robert stumbled up the narrow staircase to their room it was dark both outside and inside the lodging house. And it was numbingly cold.

"There will be a hard frost tonight, boys," Mistress Corrie, their landlady, had observed when they had arrived at her door. The darkness had covered Robert's appearance, and it had not been necessary for him to speak. Sam had agreed with Mistress Corrie that it was indeed very cold and that the river would probably freeze. Then he and Robert had escaped, feeling their way up the stairs to the room they had shared with William for almost a year.

It was hardly warmer there than it had been outside. Sam helped Robert to a stool, and, groping for the tinderbox, lit a candle. Then he took the blanket from Robert's bed.

"Sit there, Robert, and warm yourself as best you can," he said, removing his friend's cap and wrapping the blanket round his shoulders. "When William comes, one of us shall go out for bread."

"Cannot eat," mumbled Robert.

Sam sat down beside his friend on another stool. He held up the candle. Its light showed a strained expression in Robert Goughe's familiar, wide-apart eyes, his pockmarked complexion, and the ridge in his hair where his cap had been pulled low over his brow. But his mouth was still covered with the bloodstained shirt. "Let me see your injuries," coaxed Sam. "And you must tell me how you got them. If Mr Allen has anything to do with this, Mr Shakespeare and Mr Burbage should know."

"Was not Mr Allen!" This protest caused Robert much pain, and he groaned. "An accident. Need a drink, Sam."

Sam went to the pitcher in the corner and poured ale into a drinking vessel. "You will be no use in *Much Ado* if you cannot speak," he told his friend. "Mr Shakespeare must know of this so that he can hire a replacement. Here, rinse your mouth."

Sam held out a bowl. Tenderly, Robert removed the shirt-bandage and took the cup from Sam's other hand. When he saw Robert's mouth, Sam gasped. "In the name of God, what happened?"

The injury was not the kind caused by a blow from a fist, or a fall on to a hard object. It was, as surely as Sam lived, a deep cut from a knife. Even, perhaps, a sword.

At that moment a noise was heard on the staircase. Robert hastily covered his mouth again, but when William flung open the door he lowered the shirt and took a sip of the water. Sam and William stared at him. Unable to swallow, unable to spit into the bowl, Robert's head lolled backwards while the thin brew, mingling with his blood, ran down his swollen chin and on to his shirt collar, stiff with reddish-brown stains.

"Help me, William," said Sam. "We must get him to his bed and summon help. This is worse than I had feared."

"Has he been fighting?" asked William.

"I do not know."

The two boys managed to lift Robert's inert body. They laid him down and propped up his head. William examined Robert's hands and forearms. "There are no signs that he has defended himself, Sam. Someone has attacked him unawares," he concluded. "Our masters must hear of this."

"Robert wants it given out that it was an accident. He fears further violence if he tells the truth."

William looked down at the figure on the bed. Robert's face had grown pale. His eyes were closed. "We must help him," said William. "One of our masters will pay for a surgeon."

The boys looked at each other. "Mr Heminges," suggested Sam, "is a friend to the apprentices. Mr Shakespeare said so only today."

William seemed doubtful. "He may help us, to be sure, but he will see as clearly as we do that this is the work of a determined villain."

"But he is no fool," returned Sam. "He will not tell of his suspicions. Now, I will hasten to his house and return with a surgeon within the hour. You keep Robert warm."

"If I am to keep him warm you must bring more blankets," declared William stoutly. "And get more candles if you can. One of us must watch all night."

Sam ran. The streets were slippery with fast-forming frost, but he cared little for his safety. He had recognized the damp pallor of Robert's skin: he had seen it when his brother Thomas, Clarice's twin, had lain on the bed he had shared with Sam, dying from an axe wound. That had been a truly accidental injury, inflicted by Thomas himself while chopping wood. As Sam's father had tried in vain to staunch the blood, Sam had watched the life go out of his brother's eyes. He was determined that would *not* happen to Robert Goughe. The man who had done this, whoever he was, would not get away with murder.

"Mr Heminges! Mr Heminges, sir!" he called, knocking on the closed shutters of the window. "It is I, sir, Sam Gilburne. Come to the door yourself, sir, if you please!"

He waited, shivering, while bolts were shot and keys turned.

"Are you mad, boy?" asked Mr Heminges, a glass of wine in his hand, a fur-lined cloak around his shoulders and his young wife behind him. "It is cold enough tonight to freeze hell itself."

Then he saw the trembling of Sam's lips, from agitation and cold, and hastened him indoors. "For pity's sake, what is it? Rebecca, bring more wine, then leave us."

Breathlessly, Sam explained. As Mr Heminges listened his eyes grew narrow. "Pale and helpless, you say?"

"Yes, sir."

"There is no time to drink wine. Let us go immediately, and knock up Master Pollard on the way. He overcharges me for trimming my beard, but has a worthy reputation as a surgeon. Let the scoundrel earn his money for once."

"If you please, sir, can Mistress Heminges spare a blanket or two?"

Mr Heminges looked at him, exasperated. "You apprentices … anything else?"

"Candles?"

Under the red and white sign of the barber-surgeon, Mr Pollard's displeasure at being called out was tempered by the coins Mr Heminges pressed into his hand. "Now, Pollard, without delay," he instructed the surgeon. "Follow me and this lad, and bring your pack."

As Sam had secretly feared, even the best efforts of Master Pollard could do little to help Robert. The surgeon bandaged the wound, tut-tutting over it, but, as his profession often demanded, asking no questions. "Nature will take its course," he said solemnly when he had finished. "Sit with him tonight, keep him warm and give him a drink when he is able to take it. But remember, if a fever starts, send for a physician."

"Send for a mortician, more like," said William gloomily after Mr Heminges and the surgeon had departed. "Did you know, Sam, that it was a fever that killed Mr Shakespeare's own son?"

Sam had not known this. "It must have been before I joined the company," he said. "I confess, I did not even know Mr Shakespeare had any children."

"The boy was his only son, though he has two daughters," explained William. "They live with his wife in the country. He seldom sees them."

"And never speaks of them, it seems," said Sam.

"True, but he carries his grief in his heart. I have seen him weep when something reminds him of his loss."

Sam pondered. Mr Shakespeare's wife and children might live far away, but tears for a dead son spoke of an attachment unaffected by distance. "How old was the boy?" he asked.

"Only eleven. His name was Hamnet, and he was the twin of Mr Shakespeare's daughter Judith, who is nearly fourteen now."

These words struck Sam. His sister Clarice had also lost her twin brother when they were eleven. She was also fourteen years old. Had Mr Shakespeare and Sam's father spoken of their recent identical tragedies that day, three years ago, when Sam had begun his apprenticeship? Or did each man, in William's words, carry his grief in his heart?

"Sam," William was saying, "does this not make you wish you were a gentleman, who carries a sword and can avenge an injury to his friend?"

"I have no desire to be anything other than plain Sam Gilburne, a player in the Lord Chamberlain's Men," said Sam. He paused, and looked at William. "Though I must say, revenge would be sweet."

"I will wager that a gentleman like Lord Essex would have no hesitation in issuing a challenge," said William decisively. "And neither would my Lord Southampton – now *that* is a swordsman."

"And a poet," added Sam. "Mr Shakespeare admires his work greatly."

"As well he might. And Lord Southampton is wealthy enough to be a generous patron of the Lord Chamberlain's Men. God has smiled on him, to be sure."

"Aye, and he is a man of fashion too. Mr Shakespeare's hat, the one with the feather you like so much, was a gift from Lord Southampton, I believe."

Both boys were silent. Both looked at their friend's pale face on the pillow. Their thoughts turned to the same thing, and they regarded each other gravely. Sam was the first to speak.

"We do not need to be men of wealth and fashion, or wield swords, William. Our revenge upon Mr Allen is laid out before us as plainly as Robert is laid on this bed. The Lord Chamberlain's Men shall get The Theatre back from that – what did Mr Kempe call him? – that grasping blockhead. Not by force, but by the use of our wits."

It was crowded at Mistress Turville's alehouse. The combination of snowy weather and Christmastide had driven more patrons than usual to take refreshment there. When William pushed open the door he and Sam were greeted by a fog of pipe smoke and the sharp stink of bodies. Sam felt the breath almost squeezed out of him as he pushed his way through the close-packed revellers, following William to the room at the back where meetings of the Lord Chamberlain's Men were always held. Inside, there was barely room around the table for Sam to wriggle his own shoulders between William's narrow ones and the broader frame of Mr Richard Burbage.

"How now, Master Sam," said Mr Burbage, who, awe-inspiring on-stage, never struck Sam as anything but amiable in other circumstances. "And how fares the stout-hearted young Goughe?"

"Much better, I thank you, sir," said Sam. "He is able to take a little soup, and his wound is healing well. He will bear the scar till the end of his days, though."

"And he will tell a different story of its origin to every woman he woos, no doubt."

"No doubt, sir," said Sam obediently.

Mr Shakespeare called the meeting to order. "Gentlemen," he said, standing up and removing his hat, which he held to his chest like a penitent in church. "I stand before you as a poor player, simple and ignorant…"

He had to stop. His words had brought from the company a roar of indulgent protest. "Very well," he went on as soon as he could, "I stand before you as a humble penman. A poet and a playwright, whose needs are few."

Again, a roar. And another "p", for performer, thought Sam.

"The greatest of those needs is a place in which to show my plays," said Mr Shakespeare, his bright eyes taking in every man present. "Do you not agree, my loyal friends, that we need a permanent theatre, belonging to *us*?"

A great cheer arose, accompanied by the stamping of fists upon the table and boots upon the floor.

"Then I call upon my illustrious friend to reveal how we are to obtain it," said Mr Shakespeare. He gestured with his hat towards Mr Cuthbert Burbage, and sat down amid applause.

Mr Cuthbert Burbage, though no actor, had been a sharer in the company a long time. He was used to appearing before the half-drunk, rowdy and expectant collection of actors, apprentices, wardrobe and properties masters, stage managers and stage hands he now faced. He stood up.

"Today is Christmas Day," he announced. "Over the past week, events have moved on apace. We – that is myself and my fellow sharers in the Lord Chamberlain's Men – have secured a site on which to build a new theatre. It is on the south side of the river, in South-wark, near the playhouse known as the Rose, where the Admiral's Men play."

"But the Admiral's Men are our rivals!" declared Mr Kempe scornfully. "How will building a new theatre next to theirs profit us?"

"And what are we to build it *with*?" added Mr Armin. "Our wages for the next ten years?"

"Gentlemen, temper your anxiety awhile," said Mr Cuthbert Burbage. "The site is a worthy one, I assure you, Mr Kempe. And we intend to build the new theatre with the remains of the old."

There was a baffled silence. Every eye was on the speaker, every ear alert to his next words.

"Believe me, all of you, I am correct," Mr Burbage continued. "Mr Allen owns the *land* The Theatre is built on, but my brother and I lease the *building* from him."

There were some gasps, then Mr Kempe slapped the table. "Have you taken leave of your senses, Cuthbert? Everyone knows that if you build upon another man's land you will lose the building to him!"

"But not," replied Mr Burbage steadily, "if you steal the building from the land. We cannot take away Mr Allen's land, but we *can* take away The Theatre. And we will. We are going to pull it to pieces and use the materials to build the new theatre in Southwark."

Everyone began to talk at once. Mr Kempe won the battle to be heard. "But will Mr Allen's lawyers not attempt to stop us?"

"Mr Allen's lawyers," said Mr Burbage, with some satisfaction, "can do nothing to alter the terms of the lease."

"But he also has henchmen who will not shrink from causing 'accidents' to befall people," observed Mr Heminges. "We must be very careful how we proceed."

Sam voiced the question he was sure everyone wanted to ask. "And how are we to take the building to pieces without Mr Allen preventing us?"

"Mr Allen will know nothing about it," replied Mr Burbage. "He has gone away for Christmas. By the time his lawyers are sober again it will be accomplished."

Mr Shakespeare leaned forward, his palms on the table, his eyes alight. "We perform *Much Ado About Nothing* at court tomorrow. Then we have no more performances until we present *A Midsummer Night's Dream* before the queen at the palace on New Year's Eve. Mr Allen will not return until the New Year festivities are over." His gaze took in all those gathered at the table. "Men, I hope you are strong in body as well as spirit. We are to dismantle a building which holds two thousand people, and have only four days in which to do it."

Whenever Sam saw Queen Elizabeth he marvelled at two things. How imposing she continued to look despite her frailty, and that he, Sam Gilburne, player apprentice and son of a yeoman farmer, was here in the Long Chamber of the Palace of Whitehall, looking at her.

Surrounded by her ladies-in-waiting and her chief gentlemen courtiers, she sat on a dais at one end of the chamber, directly before the stage. Sam knew that he owed his livelihood to Her Majesty's love of plays. Though the administration of theatres was in the hands of the Master of the Revels, everyone knew that many of his actions originated with the queen. Yet the royal foot never graced any of the theatres of which she was such a champion. It was at court, away from the public gaze, that the queen wished the Lord Chamberlain's Men to entertain her.

She wore white make-up, like Sam and the other boys did on stage, and red dye on her lips. Gentle-women's complexions were supposed to look white in order to be beautiful, although Sam liked equally well to look at the naked faces of lesser-born women in the street, or in the audience at the theatre. But fashion was fashion, and where the queen led, ladies were bound to follow.

On the queen's frizzy hair, which was really a wig, nestled a golden coronet set with pearls. More pearls draped her neck, framed by a stiff collar more enormous and more ornate than any Sam had seen her wear before.

How many seamstresses had it taken to make her silken gown, with its jewel-bedecked skirt and sleeves? How many lacemakers to shape that collar, and maids to starch it? How many ladies-in-waiting were needed on an occasion like this, to dress Her Majesty in this finery?

Sam smiled to himself as he awaited his cue, thinking of the frantic, scrambled minutes he and the other apprentices had between scenes to don, doff or change the layers of clothing a woman wore. Sometimes there was no time to take off the man's shirt worn by their previous character. So a woman's corset, her hooped farthingale, her petticoat and underskirt, the accursedly uncomfortable stomacher, scarcely needed to flatten a boy's front, but necessary for the illusion, then the gown, the sleeves, the ruff, and sometimes a cloak and hat, had to be flung on as quickly as possible over it. And if he did not have time to put on women's shoes, Sam would have to go on stage still wearing men's boots under his skirt.

This evening he was dressed as Hero, in crimson velvet. In this performance he was not required to double as anyone else, so his head-dress was still on straight and the starch in his collar had not yet begun to melt. The room, heated by a fireplace at each end and lit by a thousand candles, was stifling. Perspiration mingled with the white make-up that caked Sam's face. He could see streaks appearing in William's too, as his friend's high-heeled shoes kicked his skirt out of the way of his next move, a comic, though complicated, sequence of hat exchanging.

It passed off perfectly, and when William came off to loud applause, Sam saw in his blue eyes the satisfaction of another hazard safely navigated. They grasped each other's right hand, grinning. The performance was the best they had ever done of *Much Ado About Nothing*.

"I like this play exceedingly well, Will," the Earl of Essex told Mr Shakespeare in Sam's hearing, when the players were gathered around the supper table laid for them in a separate room. In the Long Chamber dancing was now beginning, but Lord Essex and other aficionados of the theatre had followed the players. "Might you not play it at Essex House one day?"

Mr Shakespeare bowed. "We would be honoured, my lord."

"When I return from Ireland, perhaps?"

Mr Shakespeare bowed again. "As you say, my lord."

"Come, Will, away with this damned bowing and my-lording," said Lord Essex impatiently. "You may ask me if I have succeeded in securing the Irish commission, since I am sure every gossip in London wishes to know."

"In that case, sir, I will."

"And in that case, I can tell you that I have. Her Gracious Majesty has seen fit to bestow on me the honour of leading her army against the Irish rebellion. I set sail in March."

"Congratulations, my lord," said Mr Shakespeare. He did not bow again. "You will doubtless do England and Her Majesty proud."

"Thank you for those loyal words," said Lord Essex.

"Your Lordship will always be sure of the friendship of the Lord Chamberlain's Men," returned Mr Shakespeare. "Not merely as long as you remain one of our respected supporters, but beyond that to the grave."

Robert Devereux, Second Earl of Essex, his nobly shaped features surrounded by dark hair worn fashionably long and curled, Sam supposed, by curling tongs, looked at Mr Shakespeare seriously for a moment. Then his eyes began to shine in the way familiar to Sam from other court occasions and the many times Lord Essex had joined the company at the playhouse and at Mistress Turville's.

"Let us hope the grave is prepared for a long wait for an occupant," he said. "And, meanwhile, let me toast your players, who have given us such accomplished entertainment this evening." He held up his glass. "To the Lord Chamberlain's Men! And to Mr William Shakespeare, the foremost playwright in England!"

Sam and William drank the toast, then Sam poured himself some more wine from a pitcher on the table. "Poor Robert will be mortified to have missed this," he said, taking a gulp. "It is the best wine I have ever tasted."

"Let us hope it is not the strongest," observed William, "or you will pass out and I will have to carry you home. Not for the first time, either."

"Nor the last, I hope," said Sam happily.

He drained the glass, throwing his head back. When he lowered it again, noticing that a pleasant glow had begun to affect his vision of the room, he became aware that a gentleman stood before him, shaking his head and laughing. "Drunken apprentices? What will your master say?"

With one movement Sam and William bowed to Henry Wriothesley, Third Earl of Southampton. "I will make sure my friend Sam does not bring the company into disrepute, my lord," said William solemnly.

Lord Southampton, whom Sam strongly suspected was prevented only by his high birth from joining the company himself, laughed louder. "Disrepute! Were the Lord Chamberlain's Men ever in anything *but* disrepute? The day I hear otherwise I shall withdraw my patronage, Master Hughes."

Neither Lord Essex nor Lord Southampton ever showed the apprentices any hauteur, nor did they expect sycophancy. Their conduct was the same to them as it was to all the members of the Lord Chamberlain's Men – conscious of their own superior position, but free, good-humoured and fair. Sam was thankful that he was serving his apprenticeship among those who considered the ill-treatment of boys to be as ungentlemanly as the ill-treatment of women. In other professions, he knew, it was not always so.

"Did you enjoy the play, your lordship?" asked William, smiling.

"I enjoyed it excessively, I thank you," said Lord Southampton. He widened his eyes at William. "But who could not enjoy the sight of the lady Beatrice portrayed by Master Hughes, whose beauty is scarcely less striking than that of a true woman?" Then he turned to Sam, who felt dizzy and wished to sit down, but could not do so in their lordships' presence. "Do you not agree, Master Sam, that you are privileged to lead your life in the company of such pulchritude?"

Sam leaned against the edge of the table. Even if his wits had not been blunted by wine, he would not have known what pulchritude was. He could only assume that it was complimentary to William. "Yes indeed, my lord," he said.

Sighing, Lord Southampton placed one hand on each of William's shoulders. Thus imprisoned, William awaited the outcome of the earl's action with his usual nonchalance. Sam felt a strong desire to be elsewhere. He did not disapprove of certain men's enslavement to his friend's pulchritude, whatever that was, but he was always relieved that he himself did not excite such attention. Also, his dizziness had turned to nausea.

"Excuse me, my lord," he said, putting his weight on his feet. "I fear I am unwell."

"Go, go, boy," said the earl, his eyes still on William's face. "And when you have finished displaying the contents of your stomach to the world, wipe your mouth and sample the banquet!"

Sam rushed for the spittoons at the side of the room. Surprisingly, he did not vomit. Sweat beaded his forehead, and he felt cold, but the wine stayed in his stomach. He managed to recover his dignity – nobody of any consequence was nearby – and reached for the nearest chair. Slumped in it, he nibbled a piece of bread, feeling foolish but not miserable. The euphoria of the performance would take a while yet to wear off. Meanwhile, the bread would soak up the contents of his stomach, and he would begin to feel well again.

It was while he was thus engaged that something quite unexpected happened. When he looked back on it, as he did many times after that evening, he could not have wished it any different. It was perfect, and not merely because he was seeing everything from a beneficial, wine-induced perspective.

A girl appeared at the open door of the room. Framed by the carved portal, with the darkness of the hallway behind her, and the brightness of the room illuminating her golden gown and the jewels in her hair, she appeared to Sam like a work of art.

He gazed, transfixed, uncaring if anyone saw him. To be present at this evening's entertainment so richly attired, the girl must be of noble birth. She was slender, and her skin was so naturally pale that she had no need of the white pigment worn by older ladies. Dark hair, parted in the middle under a lace-trimmed cap, shone in the candlelight as brightly as her jewels.

Nervously, her eyes darted about the company. She could not come in, since it was not considered seemly for ladies to mingle with the players. She was looking for someone. Sam, though emboldened by the drink, knew that the social divide between them was too great for him to speak to her. But he rose to his feet and went on looking at her.

Suddenly, she noticed him. Her eyes halted in their quest. Her face became very still, the lips placed carefully together, the eyelids wide open in their smooth sockets, the pearl-drop earrings motionless. Sam did not sit down again. Silently, he looked back. And, for want of an alternative, she spoke to him.

"I am looking for Lord Essex. Do you know if he is in this room?"

Now that she had spoken Sam could reply. "He is, my lady. I will fetch him to you. Who shall I say…"

"He is my uncle," the girl announced stiffly, colour coming into her cheeks. Custom decreed that she must treat Sam, an apprentice, as she would a manservant. "Tell him Lady Lucie is looking for him. My aunts and I are about to take our leave."

Sam bowed. Lord Essex's niece might command him as she wished. She was, without any possible doubt, the most beautiful girl he had ever seen. And if pulchritude *were* a complimentary word, then she was surely the most pulchritudinous person a man had any right to behold.

The Theatre

$\mathcal{D}$arkness lay over London. The darkness of a long, impenetrably cold winter night. Frost had crisped the thick snow, and the mere act of walking was treacherous. Unsurprisingly, the midnight streets of Shoreditch were deserted.

But into this frozen world crept those whose future livelihood depended on tonight's adventure. Sam, placing his feet numbly in the footprints left by the larger ones of Mr Richard Burbage, was careful not to fall and drop the pickaxe he carried over his shoulder. The weight of it reminded him of how he had carried a scythe at home, following another line of men and boys, not over frozen snow, but across grass-scented fields, to bring in the harvest. Everyone had helped, from his eldest brother Edward to his smallest sister Anne. He remembered the first year he had been told to wield the scythe. Thomas had died that winter, leaving them short of hands, and Clarice had cried when she saw him shoulder it.

The head of the procession stopped. In the light of Mr Burbage's lantern Sam saw the hulking shape of the theatre rising from the snowy ground. Its walls looked thick and impassable, its roof very high. For a moment Sam felt excited, like an armoured knight of the Crusades, faced with a mighty citadel seething with heathen armies. But as more lanterns were lit and flares stuck in the snow, he remembered that there was no armour and no heathen army. There was only the Burbages and their mother, whose determination to see Giles Allen outwitted was as great as her sons', and the Lord Chamberlain's Men. Mr Shakespeare had excused Robert, of course, and also Mr Kempe, whose legs and chest would stand neither the work nor the cold. But everyone else, and any able-bodied man whose loyalty to the cause was proven, had assembled promptly at midnight. They now gathered round Mr Richard Burbage.

"It is the timbers we must get," he instructed. "Once they are exposed, my builders will come with carpenters and winch them away. We must begin now, so that by daylight the walls will be breached and the building beyond use. Come, men, to work with your picks and spades!"

It was exhausting work. Sam sank his axe repeatedly into the plaster walls of the building in which he had performed so many times, tearing it away, making one hole and then another. Others all around him were doing the same. Gradually, the huge timbers which formed the frame of the playhouse became visible – solid, a foot square at least, planted deep in the ground like the oak trees they were made from. Sam wondered if Mr Burbage's calm prediction that carpenters would "winch them away" would prove over-confident. The building had stood for more than twenty years, protected by these wooden posts against every storm, every harsh winter, every one of the millions of uncaring footsteps that had tramped and stamped on its floors. Was it truly going to submit so easily to the ravages of a horde bent on its destruction?

The answer soon became clear. Like the Arabian citadels of old, the theatre was besieged by men fired with their conviction of the justness of their cause. Unlike those citadels it had no one to defend it. By the time the sun rose over the roofs of Shoreditch, the building had succumbed. Large holes had appeared between all its uprights, and a scaffold was going up to allow the dismantling of its roof. Its old-fashioned outside staircases led to nothing but forlorn, exposed posts, and its galleries looked down on growing piles of rubble.

Astonished residents gathered. Some, when they heard the story, became immediate supporters of the Burbages. They fetched tools, calling for their wives and daughters to bring food and drink for the weary workers. Others, however, surveyed the scene with graver countenances. Just after midday a representative of Mr Allen arrived on horseback, his cloak flying.

"Which is Mr Cuthbert Burbage?" shouted the horseman.

"Here." Mr Burbage came forward. "To what do I owe this pleasure, sir?"

Dismounting, the horseman proffered a rolled-up paper. "You are charged, Burbage, with trespass and criminal damage."

Mr Burbage took the paper and dropped it into the rubble. "I understand the charges, sir," he said loftily. "But who are you to deliver them?"

"I am Mr Aubrey Sillitoe of this parish. I am an attorney at law," announced the man. "What say you to the charges?"

"I say that if you, Mr Silly Toe, are acting on behalf of Mr Giles Allen, then you had best begone," replied Mr Burbage. "Mr Allen has no right to accuse me. I am not on his land. I am on the public highway, just as you are yourself, sir, and your mighty steed."

As he said this he patted the nose of the horse, which was an ageing mare. The incensed Mr Sillitoe drew breath to speak, but Mr Richard Burbage, who had appeared beside his brother, spoke first.

"The true owner of a building such as this, sir, would not have neglected it as Mr Allen has done. A worthy man would not quibble over a lease rightfully bequeathed from my father to my brother and myself. And if you are indeed an attorney at law, Mr Sillitoe, you will know that it is a risky business, having other men lease a building on your land. Now be off with you, and send no more messengers from a defeated man. We are too busy to feel either fury or pity."

During this exchange Mr Shakespeare had been standing in the shadow of a staircase, his arms folded and his boots wound with straw against the wet. He looked like the brigand the Master of the Revels thought he was. When the attorney had gone he advanced. "A worthy speech, Richard," he said to Mr Burbage, "delivered as nobly as any speech I have written for you. And clever, too, as the risky business is ours, not Giles Allen's."

The day wore on. By four o'clock, under heavy clouds and falling snow, the builder's men had succeeded in dismantling the first of the timbers. Carts began to transport them away from the site.

"Where are they going?" William asked Mr Heminges.

"Do not ask. When we are able, we will take them to their new home on the other side of the river."

"And how long will it be before the new theatre is ready?" asked Sam.

"That is in the hands of the builder," replied Mr Heminges. "But Mr Burbage is confident that we shall be performing there by the summer. Now, I think we have performed excellently in quite a different capacity today, and deserve our rest. An early start again tomorrow, boys, remember."

As darkness fell once more over the city, Sam and William trudged wearily back to Mistress Corrie's house. For the fiftieth time since William had shaken him awake in the darkness, which seemed like a hundred years ago, Sam thought about the girl he had seen at the palace. Lady Lucie, he said to himself. Lord Essex's niece, who might again attend the palace with her uncle.

"When do we next perform at court?" he asked William.

"In three days' time, on New Year's Eve. *A Midsummer Night's Dream*."

"I am Hermia in that," said Sam, dismayed. This was one play he might not have wished Lady Lucie to attend. In the script Hermia was called "little" and "puppet", and even "dwarf". "It is a part designed to make me look foolish."

"True. And very funny it is, too," said William. "But do not fret, my pretty one, since it has been decided that Nathan Field, who is even shorter than you, will play Hermia. As Robert is indisposed, you must be Helena instead."

"So I must!" said Sam with relief.

William gave him an interested look. "Why are you so pleased? Robert's injury has put everyone to inconvenience."

The snow began to fall in larger, faster flakes. "My feet are soaked," said Sam. "And I was never so tired in my life." He pulled his cap lower and his collar closer, hiding his face. But William could not look at him anyway: he was defending himself from the weather equally industriously. He did not repeat his question.

In their room Robert half lay, half sat on his corner bed, his chin still bandaged but his eyes alert for his friends' arrival. "What news?" he asked.

William gave a vivid version of the day's events. He and Sam, glad to amuse Robert, acted out the confrontation between Mr Burbage and the attorney. William embellished it with curses neither gentleman had used, and Sam objected, and William told him he was a saucy pedantic wretch, and Robert, for whom smiling was painful, asked them to stop.

"I cannot laugh," he said. "But I am glad Mr Allen has lost The Theatre."

"Especially after he attacked you so wantonly," said William, looking pointedly at Robert. "It *was* him, was it not?"

Robert lowered his eyes. "It was not Allen himself," he admitted, "but one of his men. I must have made a noise, and he struck at me with his sword. I could not get out of the way. It was as you say, a wanton attack."

"But a wanton attack," concluded Sam with satisfaction, "now rightfully avenged. Mr Burbage says our new theatre will be ready by the summer."

William's face brightened. "I would like to be there when Mr Allen comes back and sees what we have done!" he said, rubbing his hands. "His face will be a picture!"

"You stay away from him," warned Sam. He peeled off his wet boots and stockings and inspected his red, gnarled, chilblained toes. "Fair hair and blue eyes may impress Lord Southampton, but they will have no effect on a man with a grievance."

William sat down on the bench. His eyes looked as if he were thinking about something far removed from wet feet and Mr Allen. "Robert," he said, "we play the *Dream* before the queen on New Year's Eve. Sam will be taking your place as Helena."

Robert nodded. "I know. It will be another week before I can perform, though I can come and help the dressers."

"A fine offer, my friend. But may I charge you with a further responsibility?"

"Of course." Robert's eyes fixed William's. "What would you have me do?"

"Watch over young Sam here," said William. "I would wager five sovereigns that he is up to something."

That New Year's Eve the Lord Chamberlain's Men acted *A Midsummer Night's Dream* with more than their usual verve before the queen, now that the business of dismantling The Theatre was over. So far at least, Allen's men had posed no hindrance to their plans. The building materials were safely stowed for the present in a secret place. Timbers, slates, columns, benches, doors and stair frames lay ready to make their journey to Southwark as soon as Mr Burbage judged that the danger of a lawsuit from Mr Allen had passed.

Sam had to concentrate hard on remembering his lines as Helena. Indeed, he made much use of the prompt throughout the performance. But happiness flowed through every vessel of his body as he acted the part, because there, in the second row to the side of the stage, sat Lady Lucie.

He had been aware of exactly where she was since the instant he had made his first entrance. Wearing a shimmering head-dress and elaborate ruff, she sat beside a golden-haired older lady whom Sam assumed to be her mother. She obviously liked the scenes where Mr Kempe wore an ass's head. Energetically applauding his capering, she laughed with an abandon which, to Sam, increased her beauty tenfold, though this seemed scarcely possible. And at the end of the performance she called and stamped as loudly as any of the gentlemen.

In the tiring-room afterwards Sam's heart would not rest. He put on his shirt and breeches, then took a rag and began to remove his make-up, picturing Lady Lucie the while. If he made haste, perhaps he would see her as he passed between the Long Chamber and the supper room, though she would be entertained separately, in greater style.

Robert was helping the wardrobe master fold costumes into the basket. "Were you watching the play or the audience, Robert?" Sam asked.

"Which do you consider the more entertaining?" returned Robert. He began to smile, but was soon reminded that smiling was too painful, and stopped.

"Very well, the audience. So did you see the ladies who were with Lord Essex?"

"Of course. Do you think I look at the gentlemen? I am not William, you know."

"Do you know any of the ladies' names?" asked Sam. "I have never seen the golden-haired one before. Who is she?"

"Lord Essex's sister, I believe."

Sam stopped rubbing his face. "Lady Penelope Rich?" Everyone in London had heard of this lady and her scandalous life. Married very young to Lord Rich, she had been the mistress of Lord Mountjoy for many years, and had borne him children. Could one of these children be Lady Lucie? Sam's heart gave a thud. "But does the queen not disapprove of Lady Rich?" he asked Robert. "I wonder that she is at court tonight at all."

Robert shrugged. "Lord Essex is a great favourite. If the queen desires his presence, then she will tolerate his ladies, I suppose."

Sam stood up and put one arm into his doublet while he looked for his boots. "What about the dark-haired lady, the young one, beside Lady Rich? Do you know her?"

Robert narrowed his eyes, trying to recall his view of the audience. "I do not think I have ever seen her before," he said eventually. "I thought she was mighty pretty, though."

"So did I," said Sam, pulling on his boots.

Something had occurred to Robert. He looked at Sam suspiciously.

"See you at supper, Robert," said Sam.

"Where are you going? What about the mess in here? Who is going to clear it up?"

"Well, my good friend, since you volunteered to be a wardrobe master tonight, you are," Sam told him, and left the room.

The queen had departed, and the Long Chamber was almost empty of guests. But Lord Essex and his party were still there. They clustered around the earl, laughing as he spoke. Lady Essex was not present, but Lady Rich was talking animatedly with a knot of ladies near the stage. Among them, lit by the tall candelabras each side of the dais, Sam saw Lady Lucie's dark hair and jewelled cap.

An apprentice was not supposed to linger in the presence of lords and ladies. In the supper room later, the gentlemen would congratulate Mr Shakespeare and exchange banter with the company as usual. But ladies did not do this. However attractive it might be to those of superior status, the theatre, with its undercurrents of sensuality and roguery, was exclusively a male domain. And as Lady Lucie had made clear when she had spoken briefly to him a few days ago, she considered those involved in that world – especially apprentices – to be little better than servants.

She was still beautiful, though. And as long as Sam had eyes, he could look at her. Keeping to the shadows by the wall, he stole nearer. She was inclining her head to listen to one of her companions. Sam saw the flash of jewels as she moved her small white hands. He even noticed the brightly decorated pointed shoes that peeped from under the hem of her gown.

The doors to the adjoining chamber, where supper was laid for the nobility and the musicians had already begun the first dance, were open. As the last guests moved towards them Sam positioned himself for a last glimpse of the ladies. The entrance to the smaller room where the Lord Chamberlain's Men would be entertained was close to where he stood. If anyone challenged him, he was ready to explain that he was on his way there.

Lady Lucie and Lady Rich were the last of the ladies to pass through the doorway. In the few minutes before Lord Essex and the other gentlemen followed them, something happened that seemed to Sam a little miracle, sent from God. One of Lady Lucie's pointed shoes caught in her dress. With an "Ach!" sound, she turned aside, put her hand on the doorframe to steady herself, stood on one leg and stooped to free her foot. Sam, his heart in his throat, was no more than twelve inches away.

He had not realized before how young she was. But the short distance between them showed him plainly that she could not be more than his own age, sixteen. Perhaps she was even younger. But she was of marriageable age, that was certain. And her marriageability was presumably the reason that she had been brought to Essex House, to mingle with potential suitors at court.

Irrational jealousy of those idle, rich young men with nothing better to do than pick a wife from any of the well-born families in England rose in Sam's breast. He may have considered his lowly birth before, but it had never truly troubled him. Now he was struck by the unfairness of the rules that prevented him from attempting to win the heart of this girl whose beauty and charm so stirred his blood.

He was expected to court the daughter of a man of similar rank to his own father, or perhaps of a senior player. At best he might aspire to the least marriageable daughter of an attorney or a clergyman. But attraction between men and women was no respecter of divisions, as Mr Shakespeare showed repeatedly in his plays. And if the power Lord Essex's niece exerted over him *was* attraction, would any other girl ever achieve it so overwhelmingly?

The shoe was freed, her foot was on the floor, her hand was gathering her skirt. And then she saw him.

He did not move. But necessity gave him the courage to go on looking at her. He had to. He might never see her again. Unblinking, she returned his gaze. Her eyes looked wary, yet contained a warmth he had never seen in a girl's eyes before. Her lips moved as if to speak, then she checked herself. But at the last moment before someone obscured her from Sam's view, she smiled.

Exit Lord Essex

"If my father could see me in this noxious hellhole he would turn in his grave," said Robert. "A man can barely find a piece of solid ground on which to put his feet. No one is going to come over here to see our plays."

"Nonsense," declared Sam, with more conviction than he felt. He was glad of his woollen cloak, which he wrapped close against the east wind blowing upriver. The City of London lay on the north side of the Thames. Close by where Sam sat with William and Robert, almost on the southern riverbank itself, stood the Rose, a theatre which had been there for a long time. "People come to see the Admiral's Men at the Rose," he told Robert, "so they will come to see the Lord Chamberlain's Men at the new theatre. Will they not, William?"

William looked no more persuaded than Robert of the suitability of the site, but his was not a spirit to consider defeat. "Southwark is only the width of the river away from Shoreditch, as you can see for yourself, Robert," he said mildly.

"But we and the Admiral's Men shall be in competition for the very same audience!" protested Robert.

Sam felt the truth of this, but persevered. "True, but we need employment, and our theatre has to be built somewhere," he said reasonably. "Theatres are not permitted within the city limits, as you well know."

"But *Southwark*?"

Sam looked around him. He had to concede that Southwark was not a pleasant place. Notoriously attractive to those seeking excitement and, perhaps, concealment, inns and brothels abounded. There was bear-baiting and gambling as well as other cruder entertainments. Tradesmen's premises crowded side by side with cramped houses upon the land that was not flooded by the unchecked river water. In the narrow streets, some formed by wooden bridges over deep ditches, ragged, filthy women and barefoot children mingled with men whose bent backs spoke of hard, relentless work. In the air, despite the keenness of the wind, hung the stench of animal and human waste. Sam watched an ancient woman, her encrusted skirt trailing in the mud, scouring the ditches for spoils thrown up by the murky river water.

"You will get used to it, Robert," he said. "Look over there." He pointed to the place where the foundations of the new playhouse had already been laid. "Imagine a summer scene, not under a grey sky like this, but a blue one. Imagine the flag on the new theatre fluttering, and music playing, and the smell of the food stalls, and the crowds alighting from the ferries. They will be coming to watch *us*."

"And what will we be doing? A very strange new play, Nathan Field says," returned Robert.

He looked very cross. The scar on his chin was yet raw, but he had begun to act again the week after New Year, thick white make-up hiding the evidence of the attack.

"Strange in what way?" enquired William.

"It is about Julius Caesar," Robert informed them. "Nathan says it is full of portents and predictions and the like. It sounds to me like a risky sort of play to be opening with. Cannot we do *Romeo and Juliet*? Everyone likes that one."

"Have faith in Mr Shakespeare," advised William.

"Am I also to have faith in Mr Burbage, when he says the theatre will be ready by the summer?"

Sam had pondered on the same question, but did not betray this. "Of course," he said. "The builders are confident it will be finished in May."

"But here is March, and they have only built the foundations," observed Robert. "Builders are pleased to make happy forecasts, my father always used to say, whether they can meet that date or no."

"I wish *you* would be pleased to make happy forecasts!" cried Sam, his patience exhausted. "We cannot do anything to change either the writing of the play or the building of the theatre, so we must leave it to our elders and be done."

Robert sighed, and nodded. "Would I had your trust, Master Sam." He rose and stood beside his friends, and all three boys looked across the river to the roofs of the city, above which rain-clouds were gathering. "We should make haste to the dockside," said William, "if we are not to arrive there after it is all over."

The Lord Chamberlain's Men had been granted a day of freedom. There was no performance that March afternoon, and Mr Shakespeare had not called a rehearsal. He knew that the players, along with many other London citizens, would prefer to make their way to Tilbury Dock to watch Lord Essex's departure for Ireland.

The river was crowded, but William managed to hail a boat. "Tilbury?" asked the boatman.

"Of course," replied William amiably as the boys climbed in. "Along with every other eastbound boat, by the looks of it. There will be thousands on the dock."

"For myself, I consider Lord Essex to deserve the best send-off the citizens of London can give him," said Robert emphatically. "He is the noblest gentleman living in England. You agree with me, Sam, do you not?"

Sam thought about Lord Essex. He thought about his long-held position as the favourite of all the queen's courtiers. He thought about the great wealth he was reputed to have amassed from the plunder of foreign ships. But fame and riches were not enough, it seemed, for Robert Devereux. He wanted to be a military hero too. The rewards that awaited him if he succeeded in quashing the Irish rebellion were great. But the queen had given him this commission only reluctantly, by all accounts. Lord Essex may have shown courage on previous campaigns, but he was also notorious for extravagance and greed. Her Majesty had recalled him in the past, and would show no scruple in recalling him again.

"I admire Lord Essex, certainly," he said. "Especially for his support of the theatre. Indeed, do you not sometimes think that both he and Lord Southampton would prefer to tread the boards of our stage rather than the floors of the Palace of Whitehall?"

"They are welcome to join us," laughed William, "if they can act like Mr Burbage, sing like Mr Armin and dance like Mr Kempe!"

The spectators at Tilbury Dock were packed as closely as the groundlings at a popular play. William, Sam and Robert forged a way through the crowd until they reached a place with a good view of the waiting ship. The wind was stronger than it had been upriver. "I wish we had brought something to eat," said Robert. "I am famished fit to faint."

William was scanning the scene before them. "Did you know that Lord Southampton accompanies Lord Essex to Ireland as master of the horse?" he asked. "It is rumoured that the appointment was made not by the queen, but by Lord Essex himself. I wonder if she would have chosen to send them to Ireland together."

"Why not?" asked Robert. "Surely Her Majesty would not deny a man the companionship of his friend on a dangerous mission?"

"But when such friends accompany each other abroad, Robert…"

Sam knew why William could not finish. Advancing age had not weakened the queen's resolve to eradicate all possibility of rebellion. She had succeeded in retaining both the throne and political power for many decades, and would do so until her death. Among the crowd that pushed and pulled the boys on the quayside, and looking no different from other men and women, there would be spies, ready to take any hint of intrigue back to the queen's advisors. It was inadvisable to express an opinion on Lord Essex's defiance of Her Majesty in private. In public, it was verging on dangerous.

"Look, masters!" cried Robert, pointing, his next words obliterated by the cheers of the spectators.

As the afternoon turned to dusk the entourage appeared. Lord Essex, on a fine bay, was followed by his squire, also mounted, his menservants and pages on foot, and porters carrying his personal luggage. The crowd, their long wait forgotten, cheered and cheered. Lord Essex knew his own popularity and received it shamelessly. But Sam was more interested in the open carriage that followed his entourage. Three women sat in the carriage: Lord Essex's wife Lady Frances, his sister Lady Penelope Rich, and Lady Lucie.

Three months had passed since New Year's Eve. The players had not been invited to perform at Essex House, but Sam never tired of the thrill of anticipation he felt every time he made his first entrance upon the stage at the Curtain theatre, and glanced at the place where Lord Essex habitually sat. It was always in vain. But fine ladies were notoriously shy of winter weather, he told himself, and the gallery of the Curtain was not well protected from rain and wind. Perhaps, when the new theatre opened in the summer, Lady Essex or Lady Rich would bring Lady Lucie there.

These thoughts passed through his head as he gazed and gazed. Lady Lucie's cape was trimmed with fur. All the ladies wore hats of the highest fashion, Lady Lucie's having a tall plume that shivered with the movements of her head. How happy she looked! Sam had never seen her in daylight before; her appearance tightened his stomach and shortened his breath. She had evidently escaped the smallpox, which blighted the beauty of so many girls, and the March wind had whipped a delightful bloom into her smooth, smiling countenance.

Sam stretched his neck, trying to keep the ladies in view between the heads of the other spectators. He wondered if Lady Rich really could be Lady Lucie's mother. They did not share the same features, and Lady Rich had golden hair. But she possessed Lady Lucie's alert, bright-eyed interest in whatever was going on. Sam knew that the queen had never approved of her conduct, nor of Lady Frances Walsingham's marriage to the Earl of Essex. The sisters-in-law were out of favour at court. But this did not seem to deter Lady Rich from enjoying this moment of public adoration, and she smiled broadly, turning her stylishly hatted head this way and that.

She and Lady Essex waved to the crowd. Sam waved back, feeling foolish, but unable to hide the pleasure he received from the sight of these women. He hardly noticed when another roar went up, for the appearance of the Earl of Southampton. But Robert elbowed him in the ribs, hard. "Look at Lord Southampton's horse! What would you give to have a horse of half that breeding?"

Sam watched Lord Southampton with a mixture of admiration and faint distaste. What was it about Henry Wriothesley that did not attract him? Younger than

Lord Essex by a few years, and extraordinarily well-favoured physically, he sat astride the beautiful horse with a princely air, as if the enthusiasm of the crowd was his right alone, and nothing to do with the notoriety of the man who had given him his present commission. But it was not merely this self-satisfaction that disturbed Sam. It was the artificiality of Lord Southampton's demeanour. He always looked as if he were playing a part, like the actor he wished he were.

"No wonder our master has dedicated so many of his compositions to Lord Southampton," said William, leaning close to Sam's ear and watching Henry Wriothesley with a keen eye. "Mr Shakespeare's love sonnets are not about a woman at all, you know, but about Lord Southampton. Mr Shakespeare loves him better than any woman."

Sam had often heard this kind of talk, and was unimpressed. "All poets dedicate their work to their patrons, William."

"But Mr Shakespeare has encoded the dedication, to disguise his love for him," persisted William. "He has dedicated the sonnets to 'W. H.', reversing the letters of Lord Southampton's name, Henry Wriothesley. But it fools no one. And Lord Southampton *is* a very beautiful young man, anyone can see that."

Lord Southampton, in an embroidered doublet and a plumed hat, made his slow progress through the crowds. His beauty shone out, no less iridescent than William's. Sam, pondering on this, made an observation which seemed to him transparently obvious. "*You* are a very beautiful young man too, William, and *your* initials are

'W. H.', with no reversal required."

William's immediate flush tinted his face such a bright shade of pink that Sam almost laughed. But something in the nervous movements of William's eyes stopped him. The older boy's embarrassment was too deep for ridicule.

"I wonder where Mr Shakespeare is today," said Robert. "Does he not wish to bid their lordships farewell?"

"Perhaps he cannot bear to," William said. "They are rather important to him."

Lord Essex had dismounted. Lady Essex, handed from the carriage by a manservant, joined her husband upon the quayside. They embraced, then Lord Essex held his hat high and waved it in acknowledgement of the crowd's approval. He and Lord Southampton, followed by the other noblemen who were to accompany them, and all their retinue, began to board the ship.

Lady Lucie was standing up in the carriage, holding on to the side. Beside her, Lady Rich dabbed tears. But Lady Lucie showed no emotion. Sam watched her as she waved to the departing men, her hat framing an expression of undisguised relief. For a reason Sam could not imagine, she seemed very pleased that this Irish adventure was taking her uncle away.

The Letter

They were to play *King Richard the Second* next. Sam had never liked this play, which depicted the killing of King Richard by those who wished to take over his throne. These were real events which had taken place about two hundred years ago. "I can think of twenty plays I would rather be in," he told William grumpily.

"But there are not twenty plays more popular," returned William. "Audiences like blood and treachery. And, of course," he added, with a careful look at Sam, "the play shows how fortunate we are to live *now*, in the reign of a good and gracious queen whose place on the throne is not open to challenge."

Sam's unease remained. He did not like the dark atmosphere of the play. He did not like the "blood and treachery", or any of the characters. In particular, he had baulked at Mr Shakespeare's suggestion that as well as playing the Duchess of Gloucester and a soldier, he double as Exton, the character by whose hand the king actually died. Sam knew it was only a play, and that he would only be "killing" Mr Burbage, but he had squirmed out of the part, pleading his lack of height.

"Superstitious about king-killing, are you?" William had asked. "If I had time to change my Duchess of York costume before Exton comes on to do the deed, *I* would play him."

"So would I," Robert had agreed. "Much as I admire Mr Burbage, pretending to plunge a sword into his heart would be very satisfying. And if I did it well he might give me threepence."

Sam's regret that Mr Shakespeare had decided to revive *King Richard the Second* increased when it was announced that Lady Essex would attend the performance. This news sent arrows of dread and excitement through Sam. Lady Essex was in the habit of mingling with the senior players after the performance, even when unaccompanied by her husband, in a way she could not do at court. If she were to bring her niece with her, this might present Sam with his first, perhaps his only, opportunity to be close to Lady Lucie. It was unfortunate that on her very first visit to the theatre she would see Sam in a historical tragedy, the kind of play that came least naturally to him. He was not superstitious, as William had accused him, but *King Richard the Second* was, without doubt, an unlucky choice.

On the day of the performance a thin April sun brightened the mood of the spectators as they filled the Curtain, attended as always by vendors of cakes, pies, sweetmeats and bottles of beer. Children sat astride their fathers' shoulders; women jostled one another for the best view of the stage; the galleries creaked under the weight of the many gorgeously dressed ladies and gentlemen who gathered there.

As two o'clock struck, applause broke out above the noise. Nervously, Sam watched through a crack between the curtains at the back of the stage as Lady Essex and her niece made their way to Lord Essex's usual place in the gallery. Lady Essex acknowledged with a wave the crowd's support of her absent husband. Lady Lucie, unused to such public attention, looked modestly at the floor. Sam was glad she was wearing her plumed hat, which he could easily pick out from wherever he stood on the stage.

Another roar went up when Mr Burbage, as King Richard, appeared for the first scene. The popularity of *King Richard the Second*, though incomprehensible to Sam, was undeniable. Waiting behind the curtain, he smoothed his Duchess of Gloucester costume, wishing her shoes were more comfortable, and tried to swallow his agitation.

"'Finds brotherhood in thee no sharper spur?'"

Sam's first line, spoken to Mr Heminges, came out quite satisfactorily. For all its bloodthirstiness the play was eloquent, and Sam managed to invest the Duchess's long opening speech with her lust for vengeance. He did not usually feel nervous once he had stepped on to the stage, but this afternoon his consciousness of Lady Lucie's gaze and his expectation of what might follow the performance overcame his usual serenity. He longed for the play to be over.

Mr Heminges completed his final speech of the

scene, and made to exit. Sam was supposed to call him back for "'yet one word more'". But he forgot, utterly and without any possibility of pretending otherwise, what he had to say next.

Mr Heminges, seeing the panic on his face, pretended for him. "Not one word more!" he pronounced as he left the stage.

Sam picked up the train of his skirt and followed him. He was about to voice his gratitude as they descended the stairs to the tiring-room, but Mr Burbage caught his arm. "Drying in your first scene?" he hissed. "What can be the matter with you, boy?"

"I am sorry, sir. But Mr Heminges—"

"Yes, Mr Heminges put in a line of his own, and passed off your mistake. But *I* shall not do that in my scenes with you, Sam Gilburne. There is no place in this company for a boy who has not the wit even to get through his first scene, and relies upon others to do it for him."

Sam did not dry again. But as he bowed to the audience in the soldier's costume he wore at the end of the play, he noticed that William was watching him carefully from beneath the Duchess of York's wig. "Why are you so interested today in my Lady Essex?" he asked when they came off stage. "You have not decided to fall in love with her, have you?"

Partly from irritation and partly to cover his blush, Sam cuffed William on the side of the head, dislodging his wig. "Lady Essex? Why, I should as soon have the Earl of Southampton, who is twice as pretty!"

William took off the wig and ruffled his sweat-soaked

hair. "If you were not my good friend, Master Sam, I would knock your helmet off and throw it at you."

"And I would throw it back with double the force," retorted Sam. "It is mighty heavy, you know."

"And I am mighty afraid!" mocked William. "But my curiosity is not to be denied. What is going on?"

"It is your imagination," said Sam. The blood had receded from his cheeks, but he was glad to hide under his soldier's helmet and chain-mail hood.

"It is not my imagination," insisted William.

"Very well," said Sam, trying to sound reasonable. "Do you not agree that Lady Essex, as one of our most important supporters, should be flattered with our attention at every opportunity? I would have thought *you* would be the first to understand that."

William was too intelligent to be satisfied with this explanation, but Sam was spared further questioning by the arrival of Lady Essex herself, who was handed on to the stage by Mr Heminges. Following her, requiring no help from a gentleman's hand, was Lady Lucie.

Her gaze took in the view of the theatre from the stage; Sam knew she must be imagining what it would be like to act in a play. She wore the expression he had so often seen upon the faces of high-born ladies – smooth, glossy, impenetrably superior. But she could not conceal the excitement in her eyes. Like her uncle, she was thrilled by the theatre, with its mixture of debauchery and artistry, and the delightful release it provided from the constraints which, outside the walls of the playhouse, governed everyone's life. In this company, Sam did not have to hide his admiration of

Lady Lucie's beauty. Robert nudged him and whistled softly. Even world-weary Mr Phillips, who was seldom affected by a pretty face, whispered approvingly to Mr Heminges.

Lady Essex greeted Mr Shakespeare and the other sharers with enthusiasm. "Mr Burbage!" she cried, extending her hand for him to kiss. "Another most excellent tragic performance! Do you never tire of your work?"

"Never, your ladyship," said Mr Burbage, dutifully bestowing the kiss. "A player is a player for life."

"It would certainly seem so, my good sir. Now, let me introduce my niece, Lady Lucie Cheetham," she said, bringing Lady Lucie forward. "She has implored me these three months to bring her to meet the Lord Chamberlain's Men, and Mr Shakespeare in particular."

"I am honoured, my lady," said Mr Shakespeare to Lucie. He bowed, and so did the other players. Sam took great pride in bowing especially carefully, though he knew it was next to impossible that Lady Lucie was looking at him. She made a small curtsy, her hands clasped together under her velvet cloak. "Gentlemen," she said, with a bashful smile, "I thank you all."

"Lady Lucie is the daughter of my sister and her husband," said Lady Essex. "They live far away, in Northumberland, but Lucie is staying with us at Essex House for a while." She lowered her eyes modestly. "We expect another child there in the autumn, and both Lucie and my sister-in-law, Lady Rich, will be of help to me." Looking up again, she caught Mr Shakespeare's eye. "Tell me, Mr Shakespeare, will you bring a play to Essex House when Lord Essex returns from Ireland? We have not had a performance there for many months."

Mr Shakespeare bowed again. His eyes flickered between Lady Essex and her niece. "The Lord Chamberlain's Men will do all within their power to please such fair ladies."

"Well said, sir!" cried Lady Essex delightedly. "Though my niece has a greater share of beauty than I."

During the murmured gallantry that followed this, Sam looked at Lady Lucie's smiling, blushing face, and pondered. She was not Lady Rich's daughter, then. In fact, she was not related to Lord Essex by blood at all. But her situation was as Sam had imagined. Her mother wished to display her on the marriage market, for sale to the possessor of the greatest fortune. The thought of her betrothal to an unknown rich man, perhaps many years her senior, made Sam's stomach hurt.

Lady Essex began to take her leave. Sam had taken up the usual apprentice's position, at a suitable distance from the nobility, near the door. As the ladies approached he bowed. While he was still looking at the floor, something small, square and white tumbled out from under Lady Lucie's cloak. In a flash she had put her foot on it and slid it towards Sam. Instinctively, he too concealed it under his boot. And then the ladies were gone.

Breathless, Sam crouched down, retrieved the folded piece of paper from under his boot and closed his fist around it. Then he hurried down the staircase behind the stage. Under the gallery there was a curtained space where stage furniture was stored. No one would go there immediately after a performance. In the half-light, Sam leaned against one of the pillars and unfolded the paper.

Dear Helena, or shall I call you Hero?

I know not what your masculine name is. I know only the names of those of my own sex whose words you speak so sweetly. But I have noticed you looking at me with a look I have never seen before, and which interests me greatly. I see something in it that tells me I would like you if I met you. I have many questions to ask you. Will you do me the honour of replying to this letter, and suggesting where we might meet? I promise that you can trust me. My maid, Matty, will be at the door of the theatre tomorrow at noon, to collect your letter. Tell me where you live and she will take my reply there as soon as I have written it.

God speed,

Lady Lucie Cheetham

A feverish, sweaty, uncontrollable wave of heat rushed over Sam as he read the words. Stifled by the helmet and chain-mail hood he still wore, he tore them off and read the letter again. The signature was elaborate, with the L curling round the C like a snake. His fingers trembling, scarcely knowing what he did, Sam folded the paper. He walked about blindly, stooping in the confined space below the gallery, agitated beyond anything he had ever experienced before.

He sat on the floor and unfolded the letter again. Could it be a joke? It was clear that Lady Lucie Cheetham was a joke-loving girl. When he appeared tomorrow at noon, would her maid bring a second letter from her, telling him what a fool he was?

Or was it a trick? Could it be that she was offended by his all-too-obvious attention, and had given him the note to lure him into trouble? Would he be greeted not by a maid, but a swordsman ready to challenge him to a fight?

It was cold under the gallery, but sweat pricked Sam's brow. He read the note again. Then he put it inside his boot, his mind racing. If Lady Lucie had sent it in earnest, and he did not reply, his chance to meet her would be lost for ever. Could he honestly say that the risk of ridicule, or punishment, was harder to bear than that?

She had asked him to suggest a meeting place. He tried to think. His lodging? Impossible because of Robert and William. Essex House? Impossible because of Lady Lucie's aunts. The only other place both an apprentice and a lady could legitimately go was the playhouse. But where at a playhouse, of all the buildings in London surely one of the least private, could they find any privacy?

The light had almost gone from the storage space, though five o'clock had not yet tolled. He looked around, examining the place as never before. He could not risk bringing candles down here, which was forbidden, this rule being strictly enforced by his masters. But if he could procure a lantern, a safe, enclosed lantern, why should not his present hiding-place shelter his meeting with Lady Lucie? They would have to rely upon her wits to find an excuse to come to the theatre, but he had no doubt that she was as quick as she was fair.

He hurried up the stairs, his heart drumming. Tomorrow, tomorrow and tomorrow, he thought. Why could it not be tomorrow *now*?

There she was, crouching in the dark, as bright-eyed as a cat. Sam held up the lantern, his heart ready to burst. "My lady," he whispered. "It is I, Sam Gilburne."

As he came near, and the light from the lantern illuminated her pale face and small, uncertain smile, he remembered to be suspicious. "Does anyone know you are here?"

"My Lady Rich knows I have come here to meet someone."

"Oh, no!" began Sam in alarm, but Lady Lucie shook her head.

"Fear not, she does not know *who*. I told her that Matty has asked me to help a relative of hers, a girl in trouble, whose baby's father was one of the players. I told her not to be anxious, as both the girl and the young man were to meet me under the galleries, and I intended to give them money. It is the sort of thing she would not hesitate to do herself."

Sam was impressed at her ingenuity. If her aunt caught a glimpse of him, she would assume him to be the young player who had got Matty's relative with child, and his soldier's costume from *King Richard the Second*, which they had performed again that afternoon, would hide his identity. But still he feared a trap. "Is anyone else near?" he asked. "Any of your uncle's servants?"

Her brow wrinkled, and the pink glow of

consciousness, so becoming to her, appeared in her cheeks. "My uncle's servants?" she asked, bewildered. "No! They are the last persons on earth I would want here! What can your meaning be?"

"I am wary, that is all," said Sam.

Lady Lucie's eyes glittered in the lamplight. "If you thought my note a trick, why did you reply?"

"You know why I replied."

They looked at each other. The footsteps of the departing audience clattered above their heads. "I cannot stay long," said Lady Lucie. "And by the way, we have not been formally introduced."

"Samuel Gilburne at your service," said Sam, bowing.

"Lady Lucie Cheetham." Keeping her eyes on his face, she made a low curtsy. "But I wish you to call me Lucie, as my friends and relatives do."

Sam's heart swelled. It felt so large in his chest that it stopped him uttering his next words. He swallowed them.

"I am sixteen," announced Lucie. "How old are you?"

"Sixteen." His voice had recovered, but not his composure. "I am seventeen this month."

"And I in June! We are born but two months apart!"

There was a bench near where Lucie stood. Gathering her skirts, she sat down and patted the place next to her.

"You think I am very forward, do you not, Master Gilburne?"

Sam sat down. He could not very well reply.

"My mother thinks so too," continued Lucie. "She says I have run wild in Northumberland, so she has sent me to my Lord Essex's house here in London to learn to defer to my superiors and curb my wilfulness. She says if court life will not make me behave like a lady, nothing will." She leaned towards Sam, the pearls round her neck swinging forward, the smooth flesh of her breasts pressed tightly against her bodice. Sam's blood was stirred. "Do you think," she asked sweetly, "that my mother is correct?"

Sam managed to locate his wits. "That I cannot say, my lady," he replied. "But I am sure those who have the charge of you in London will do their best to follow your mother's wishes. You, like me, are young, and are under the regulation of older people."

"I am under the regulation of no one. Lady Rich is not my blood aunt, since my mother is from Lady Essex's family, the Walsinghams. Lady Rich is living at Essex House at present, and is perfectly willing to have the guardianship of me while I am in London. But she has no interest in my *regulation*. All she is interested in is comparing young men's fortunes and inviting the richest to the house."

Sam's head felt light, as if it might blow away at any moment. But he knew he must keep his wits about him. Ladies like Lucie Cheetham were not in the habit of associating with apprentice players. There could yet be mischief afoot.

"If Lady Rich knew you were down here speaking to me, what would she say?"

Lucie broke out into laughter. "Sam, how anxious you are!" She leaned forward again. "Do not waste our precious time together in worrying. I forbid it."

"But..." Sam wondered if what he wanted to say

would offend her. However, this might be his only chance to say it. "But I do not understand, my lady. You have suitors of your own rank, and yet you chose to write to *me*, when you had only seen me a few times, and my birth is far below yours. If you were in my situation, your suspicions would be aroused, just as mine are."

"Oh!" Her colour was high, her eyes gleamed, but her smile had faded. "You do not trust me!"

"I want to trust you, Lady Lucie."

She did not immediately reply. Sam luxuriated in looking at her. Every time he had seen her she had appeared to him as if framed − by a dark doorway, a blazing hearth, a circle of lantern light. He had seen the freshness of her countenance and the richness of her clothes. But now for the first time he saw that her playful demeanour belied not only the sharpness of her intelligence, but also a private desperation.

At last she spoke, with bitterness. "Can you understand what it is like to be me? I must be courted by Lord This and Sir That, and marry whoever my family wishes, whether we are suited or no." Her beautiful eyes beseeched him. "No, you cannot understand. You are not born to such privilege!" She began to smile a little. "Most important, Sam, you have not been selected by my elders. You are young, well-favoured in looks and gifted with a skill that impresses everyone who beholds you. Ever since I saw you for the first time, I have thought of nothing but finding a way to speak to you."

Sam tried not to show his astonishment. Lucie was as enthralled by his acting skill as he was by that of his masters. "I thank you, my lady," he said humbly. "I wish only to please you."

"Now you sound like a servant!" Her smile had widened. "Do you not see how happy this makes me? For the first time in my life *I* have selected someone *I* like, who lives by his own wits and is beholden neither to his parents or his birth. How I envy you, Sam Gilburne!" She laid her hand on his. "And now, tell me you trust me."

"I do," said Sam. He was as certain as he could be that this assignation was neither a joke nor a trap, but a daring step taken by Lucie towards the freedom which was his, but not hers. "And I am honoured beyond description by your attention."

"First you sound like a servant, then you are as eloquent as a nobleman!" she laughed. "But now, tell me about *your* family."

"It is very different from yours."

"All the better to broaden my education."

"My father is a farmer. He is a yeoman of the parish. Our farm is in Sussex, near the sea. I have two brothers, Edward and Francis, and two sisters, Clarice and Anne. I left home over three years ago, when I was apprenticed to Mr Phillips. I lived in his household until last year, when William Hughes, Robert Goughe and I – they are also apprentices – took lodgings together."

"And do you like your merry little household?" she asked, playfully but not mockingly.

"They are good lads, both," said Sam. "But I often think of my brothers and sisters, especially Clarice."

"Why did you decide to be a player?"

"I saw a troupe of players perform on Horsham green," he told her. "My father was surprised when I told him what I wanted to do, but he did not object. Even without Tom, he still had three sons to find work for, and only one could take over the farm. So he took me to London and spoke to Mr Shakespeare about me."

"Were you not frightened?" asked Lucie. "How old were you?"

"Thirteen. And no, I was not frightened."

"What did Mr Shakespeare say to you?"

"He asked me if I knew my letters, and I said yes, my brothers and I had been tutored. He made me read a poem aloud. I think it must have been one of his own compositions, a sonnet. Then he had me copy it out. Then, taking the paper away from me, he asked if I could recite the first two lines. I must have said them right, because he made me sing. 'Any song,' he said, so I sang a song I had heard the ploughmen sing at home, about a lass and her swain, and a haystack. Mr Shakespeare laughed, and asked my father if I had had the smallpox, and if I was free of worms. Then he gave me a place with the Lord Chamberlain's Men, and I started the very next week."

Lucie absorbed this. Then she asked quietly, "Who is Tom?"

When Sam told her she reached for his hand. "So that is why you said 'especially Clarice'."

Sam nodded.

"It must be terrible to lose a brother," continued Lucie, "but it must be doubly terrible to lose one's twin. My heart goes out to her."

Sam's own heart felt as tight-clenched as a fist. "You are very kind, Lady Lucie."

"Lucie," she reminded him softly.

"Lucie."

They looked at each other. "I must rejoin Lady Rich soon," said Lucie.

"Will you come again to see a play?" urged Sam. "Our new theatre in Southwark is to open soon."

"I will try. But meanwhile, Matty will continue to fetch and carry our letters. Did you like Matty?"

"I saw her only briefly. She was older than I had expected."

"She is not of the Essex household. I have brought her from Northumberland with me. She has served me all my life. We may be absolutely certain of her loyalty."

"Then I will await her next delivery with impatience," said Sam gallantly.

Lucie dipped her head modestly. "And you will reply, will you not?"

"Nothing will stop me."

"You see?" she said, raising her head. "I was wrong. You *are* in my service. Not as an apprentice or a servant – no, indeed! – but as my knight. Are you about to reveal that you are an earl's son in disguise?"

"No, indeed!" returned Sam, smiling.

Lucie smiled too. "I bid you farewell, then." Her hand was still holding his. They stood up, still looking at each other. Sam saw that she was trying to memorize his features as diligently as he was trying to memorize hers. "We had better part now," she said. "I will go out, and you follow in a few minutes."

"Why, 'tis Sam Gilburne!" cried William's voice. "Robert, can you believe what you see?"

Robert, astonished, let the curtain fall behind them. Recollecting himself, he nudged William. "My lady," he said, bowing to Lucie. "We are honoured."

"Honoured," echoed William, bowing too.

Sam could not look at either of them. His face burning, he released Lucie's hand. She made a pretty curtsy to each of the boys. "You, Sir Golden Hair, must be William Hughes, and you, Sir Wide Eyes, Robert Goughe. I thank you for your courteous greeting. And I must tell you that you both look as well in your boys' clothes as you do in your girls'."

Sam saw William catch Robert's eye with an expression of wonder. Lucie turned to Sam. "I am relieved your friends have seen us. I am sure they are loyal." She turned back to William and Robert. "You are, are you not?"

They bowed obediently. "Yes, my lady," said William.

"You see, Sam? What excellent friends! And now, I must return to my aunt." She whispered to Sam that he should expect a letter tomorrow. Then she gathered her skirts and slipped round the curtain.

Sam sat down on the carved, painted chair they used for Oberon's throne in *A Midsummer Night's Dream*. His two friends stared at him with no less amazement than if he really *were* the King of the Fairies.

"Why would Lady Lucie Cheetham take it into her head to associate with *you*?" Robert asked incredulously.

"What she takes into her head is her own business," returned Sam.

"But she is Lord Essex's niece!"

"She must be deranged," observed William.

Sam bore their remarks bravely. He knew that their curiosity, their amazement, and especially their mockery, were rooted in envy. William, he suspected, had already decided that if the company of lowly Sam Gilburne were to be further sought by Lord Essex's niece, then William Hughes wanted to be beside him, ready with his delicately moulded features and flattering ways.

Robert sat down on a stool, resting his elbows on his knees and looking up at Sam. His scar still showed clearly. It had changed his countenance, Sam thought. The open-eyed candour, which so many audiences had warmed to in Robert's portrayals of girls, had hardened. He looked less trusting, as well he might.

"Deranged or not, she is a prize out of your reach, my friend," Robert said decisively.

"Does she correspond with you?" asked William.

"She does." Sam could not help colouring as he said this. The fact that Lucie had sat in her well-appointed chamber and written to him *was* astonishing, there was no denying it.

"But how are her letters delivered?" asked William.

"By her maidservant."

Robert's eyes had not left Sam's face. "You must have taken leave of your senses. There are willing wenches on any street in London. If Lord Essex finds out that you are dallying with his own niece…"

"*When* he finds out," William corrected him. "He has spies everywhere."

"...we shall all be in trouble," concluded Robert fretfully.

There was a silence. Overhead, the last footsteps of the departing crowd could be heard. Sam was still wearing his costume, more than half an hour after the end of the performance. He knew they should go back before their masters missed them, but he could not let the moment pass. He gathered his courage and spoke.

"William, hear me. And you too, Robert. When you promised Lady Lucie that you were loyal, did you speak true?"

Robert rose from his stool and parted the curtain. "What do you think?" he asked, holding it open for Sam and William to pass through. "Fool though I think you are, loyalty to a friend is no bad creed to live by."

"And neither is the love of a beautiful lady," added William as Robert let the curtain close after them. "Pursue her, Lord Gilburne of Shoreditch, and your knights will never betray you."

The Globe

The new theatre did not open in May. But before June was two weeks old, the playbills went up for *Julius Caesar*.

Robert's misgivings over the new play proved to be unfounded. The company agreed that its poetry was noble and its staging spectacular. Sam marvelled at the decorated canopy over Caesar's throne, and wondered how the wardrobe master had procured the necessary stuff for so many purple robes when the wearing of this colour remained restricted to royalty. The many night-time scenes required flares to be carried on-stage, which lent an eerie aspect to the deep shadows cast by the sun. There were trumpet flourishes, too, and drummers. And at the heart of the play lay a popular theme. Everyone liked a good conspiracy.

Sam and Robert played the only two women, Caesar's wife and Brutus's wife. Neither appeared after Caesar's death, so the boys doubled as Roman citizens for the latter part of the play. But William, to his unaffected surprise, was given the important part of Mark Antony. When questioned by Mr Phillips about this, Mr Shakespeare said calmly, "I want Mark Antony to be beautiful. The day you become more beautiful than William Hughes, Augustine, you may play the part."

They rehearsed the play a great deal. Mr Shakespeare, always a hard taskmaster, showed more than usual dedication to his art and greater shortness of temper than Sam had ever witnessed before. He demanded that they go over the important speeches many, many times, and practise their moves until no one had any hesitation. Sam, who did not have any important speeches, spent much of the time lying along the front bench of the gallery, thinking of Lucie.

It was many weeks since he had seen her after *King Richard the Second*, but Matty had brought and returned letters every few days. Lucie's letters were written in as bold a manner as she showed in person. Sam had hardly known what to write about at first, but she was interested in everything he mentioned, however trivial. Soon he began to describe his past life on the farm and his present life at the playhouse in the kind of detail he would never have thought a fine lady like Lucie would allow.

She did not mind that the people he associated with were base-born and ill-educated, or, in the case of his masters, gentlemen without family fortunes who lived by their wits and their own endeavour. She did not despise this: indeed, she admired them for it. But above all, Sam was constantly reminded as their correspondence went on, she was interested in *him*.

His heart folded at the memory of her as he had last seen her, in the lamplight under the gallery. If only he could meet her there, or anywhere, again!

"Dreaming again, Master Sam?" Mr Phillips's voice rang out from the interior space at the back of the stage. "You are wanted, boy, so wake up."

Sam went over his scene with Mr Phillips for what seemed like the hundredth time. Long though the June day was, dusk was falling by the time Mr Shakespeare called an end to the rehearsal. Even then, he seemed reluctant to let the players go.

"Gentlemen, we perform this play tomorrow afternoon at two o'clock," he told them. "It will be an auspicious occasion. I need not tell you how essential it is that the play goes well."

"Fear not, Will," said Mr Burbage, who would play Caesar. "Your work is in good hands. Now let us depart, and sleep well, and be ready on the morrow to behold the magnificent sight of our new theatre, occupied by an audience for the first time." He surveyed the men contentedly. "We have waited a long time for this day. Let us not waste it."

Sam and Robert walked to the ferry together. "Anyone would think we'd never done a play before, the way they are talking," grumbled Robert. "Have they no faith?"

"They are nervous," said Sam. "The new theatre is a big undertaking. If no one comes to see the play, their enterprise will have failed. It will ruin them, and us."

"I still think it was a mistake to build the theatre next to the Rose," insisted Robert. "The plays the

Admiral's Men do, especially Mr Ben Jonson's, are every bit as popular as Mr Shakespeare's. How can one audience suddenly become two?"

Unwilling to argue, Sam changed the subject to one that always interested Robert. "Supper will be almost ready when we get home, I expect."

"Some thin soup with not enough goodness to nourish a mouse," replied Robert gloomily.

Mistress Corrie's house was in a dark alley, slippery underfoot from the slops thrown there. Robert, unable to wait until suppertime, stopped at the baker's, and Sam approached the alley alone.

"Master Gilburne!"

Matty emerged from a doorway. She put a folded parchment into his hand. "I have not time to collect your reply, Master Gilburne. I will be missed if I am not back before dark."

"Then I will take my reply to Essex House myself."

"No!" Matty put her hand on his arm. "I will meet you tomorrow at the back door of the new playhouse at noon, and take your letter to my mistress."

She hurried away, almost bumping into Robert as he rounded the corner into the alley. Sam thrust Lucie's letter into his pocket.

"Who was that?" asked Robert, tearing bread and nibbling it. He still could not eat with abandon. "I thought I knew everyone in this neighbourhood, but I have never seen her before."

Sam was wary of telling Robert any more than he had to know. "Perhaps she has been calling on Mistress Corrie," he suggested.

"Hah! Do you think that mean old witch has any friends?"

Sam knew that once they had gone up to their room, it would not be possible to read the letter in private. "Robert," he said, "my head aches very badly. I must walk awhile, but I will come home when I hear nine o'clock strike, for supper."

"If you can call it supper."

"Will you not share your bread with us?"

"If there is any left."

Sam knew Robert would. For all his complaining, he was a simple and generous soul, given to tears when moved by poetry, a song, or fine acting. Sam trusted him as he did William. In their precarious profession, without trust there was no survival, and all three knew it.

Once out of sight, Sam leaned against the baker's shop window and opened the letter. It was shorter than usual, yet the style in which Lucie had begun it made his heart leap. Avidly, he read:

Dear, no – dearest Sam,

I have news. Lady Rich is to come to see Julius Caesar *tomorrow afternoon and I have persuaded her to allow me to accompany her. My Lady Essex is not venturing abroad at present but she has servants to tend to her needs. It is still a few weeks until she expects to be confined.*

Lady Rich has read the advertisements for this play, and tells me that it purports to treat the subject of the assassination of Caesar in a very noble but gory manner. It sounds exactly the kind of thing I thoroughly enjoy! I hope your part is played in masculine clothing, but I will be content with your

women's garb if I can see you after *the play as your real self.*
Lady Rich is to dine with Mr Shakespeare and the two Mr
Burbages at the Lord Chamberlain's house. She will offer me
the carriage, but I will dismiss it, telling the man that as the
weather is so fine (let us pray it does not break before
tomorrow!) I will go on foot with Matty. Please, please may
we meet? Write to me in great haste, telling me what to do,
and Matty will collect your letter tomorrow before the play.
I remain restless with anticipation,
      Lucie

Sam reread the letter, then folded it inside his
doublet once more. He had wished and wished to see
Lucie for over two months, but now that the
opportunity was presented to him, and she was relying
upon him to arrange the meeting, he felt apprehensive.
If Lady Rich found out that her niece was
corresponding with lowly Sam Gilburne, what would
she do? Send Lucie back to Northumberland, so that
they could never see each other again?

He tried to imagine never seeing her again.

Lady Rich or no Lady Rich, he must find a way for
them to meet, as Lucie had implored. His thoughts
racing, he turned back towards the alley. Perhaps, since
they had sworn their loyalty so faithfully, it was time to
enlist the help of Robert and William.

When William made Mark Antony's speech to the
mob after the murder of Caesar and turned them
against the assassin, the crescendo of appreciation was
the loudest Sam had ever experienced in any playhouse.

Solidly built though the theatre was, the stamping and shouting vibrated the wooden boards and echoed in the rafters as the company left the stage.

"Will, you have excelled yourself," said Mr Burbage in the tiring-room to Mr Shakespeare, who was slumped on a corner stool. "As pretty a picture of old Rome as anyone ever saw. We shall play it for years."

"Some of the Admiral's Men were in the gallery," said Mr Shakespeare. "Do you think we impressed them?"

His face betrayed the strain of months of legal battling, his anxiety about the Lord Chamberlain's Men's finances and the unending problems of the construction of the theatre at Southwark. He had even had to contend with insurrection in his own ranks. Some members of the company had wished the new theatre to be called the Phoenix, after the mythical bird that was burned, then rose from the ashes to live again, and the new theatre had so evidently arisen from destruction. But Mr Shakespeare and the Burbages had settled upon a different name: the Globe.

But today, exhausted though he was, Mr Shakespeare's eyes shone. The spirit of competition was alight in him. The public's approval was evident, but his respect for the rival company was what had pushed him to the level of achievement *Julius Caesar* represented.

"My dear Will," said Mr Burbage, laying his hand on his friend's shoulder. "I have no doubt that the Admiral's Men are gathering in some alehouse as we speak, wondering how to get their hands on material of similar worth. Ben Jonson is the only playwright in London whose work has anything like the stature of yours."

Mr Shakespeare nodded. "Aye, now that Marlowe is dead, that may be true." He leaned forward in his characteristic way, exhaustion laid aside to make way for a new thought. "Richard, my personal relief at this successful opening of the Globe shall be translated into monetary relief for my loyal men. Take a sovereign and divide it between them. Give William Hughes a shilling, and tell him that from today he is no longer an apprentice, but a hired man."

This announcement brought applause from the sharers and senior men (Mr Heminges clapped the loudest) and embarrassed delight from William. "Mr Kempe, some strong beer!" commanded Mr Shakespeare. "The Lord Chamberlain's Men shall toast this day's events, and set them in our memories for ever."

"To the Globe, and all who play in her!" he declared when every man had a goblet in his hand. "May she bring laughter and tears to all who come within her portals!"

"To the Globe!" they echoed, and drank. It *was* strong beer. Sam took another gulp.

"You were right about the name of this theatre, Will," said Mr Phillips, who had long been in favour of naming it the Phoenix. "I concede it is a good name. We *are* the world, since we put the world on our stage. Why, this afternoon we were in ancient Rome, and tomorrow – is it the *Dream* tomorrow? – we shall be in Greece. And yet we are never out of England."

"All the world is indeed a stage, Augustine," agreed Mr Shakespeare. "And all the men and women merely players. Thank you for that notion. I shall use it in a play." He raised his glass to Mr Phillips, and drank. In his face Sam saw affection, pride and, strongest of all, pleasure in the company of these men. "Now away, and dine, and end this glorious day with celebration. Mr Armin, bring the musicians. Richard, you and I and Cuthbert must hasten to meet Lady Rich. Put on your most expensive vestments, gentlemen, for we would not wish her ladyship to outdo us in finery!"

Sam sought out William and clapped him on the shoulder. "A hired man!" he cried, raising his glass. "Do you deign to speak to the likes of Robert and me now?"

"I have to," returned William good-naturedly. "I must share my lodgings with you until I can find others." He lowered his voice. "Robert has already departed. If he succeeds in his plan, all will be ready in half an hour."

Sam had never doubted William's friendship, but the meeting with Lucie under the gallery had sent the tall, blue-eyed, recently hired man's respect for the "short", "brown" apprentice several notches higher. And today, Sam was very glad of it. His brow felt sweaty, and his throat was dry. He drained his glass of beer.

William's idea was audacious, for certain. For it to work, Robert had to persuade Mistress Corrie that a gentleman of his acquaintance desired to meet her, and had requested that Robert bring his "delectable" (Sam's idea) landlady to the tavern at the sign of the lamb in Covent Garden. If all went to plan, and Robert could keep her in the tavern for exactly the right length of time, soothing her scoldings with wine when no gentleman appeared, Sam would be for ever in his friends' debt. If it did not, they might all three of them be for ever in disgrace.

"I thank you, William," he said, buttoning his doublet, "for everything."

William nodded encouragement. "Until seven o'clock, then."

"Seven o'clock," promised Sam. As he hurried down the stairs to the street he heard half past five strike. In half an hour, God willing, Lucie would be with him.

Sick with excitement, he waited in the entrance to Mistress Corrie's alley. After London had toiled under the heat of that June day, the late afternoon had brought grey clouds, though no drop of rain had yet fallen. The shade of the overhanging upper storeys of the houses obliterated all below. Every few seconds Sam looked up and down the street, shrinking back into his hiding place when each pair of approaching footsteps turned out not to be the ones he sought.

It had been William's idea to procure the Juliet cloak from the costume store. Nathan Field wore this voluminous, black, hooded cloak over his costume for the scene in *Romeo and Juliet* where Juliet came to Friar Laurence's cell to be married to Romeo. Only two years ago Sam had worn it himself, when he had still been small enough to be caught up in Romeo's arms in that most eloquent of love scenes. Juliet was a painfully poignant part to play, and it was painful to have lost it to the younger boy. But Sam had grown so fast in the last year that Mr Burbage had recently observed that he was beginning to look more clownish than girlish in love scenes. He knew his apprentice days were numbered.

Suddenly he saw it, coming round the corner by the alehouse. The Juliet cloak, being worn for the first time by a seventeen-year-old girl instead of a fourteen-year-old boy. Lucie approached, but Sam did not touch her. He did not even look at her, nor she at him. Together they entered the lodging house.

Inside it was as dark as on any winter's day. Sam felt Lucie's touch upon his wrist. He seized her hand and circled it with his fingers. Immediately, his flesh leaped into a life independent of his brain. He could not control the antics of his heart. His breath disappeared.

"Matty is waiting nearby," she said. "When we alighted from the ferry she followed a little way behind me. She chaperones me far better than my aunt, you know."

Sam took in some air. "Matty is an excellent woman," he said, hardly noticing the words, so affected was he by the scent of the oil Lucie used to dress her hair. "It is good of her to help us."

"She has no choice," said Lucie, removing the hood. In the gloom Sam saw the elegance of her neck, which even the bulky cloak could not disguise. "She is to come back when it lacks a quarter of seven o'clock. We have less than an hour, Sam. How I wish we had longer!"

Sam was glad she could not see his face very well. He was sure he was grinning like a lunatic. "So do I," he said softly. "Come now, this way."

He led Lucie up the stairs to the attic chamber. It was doubtless the lowliest room she had ever set foot in, but she did not remark upon the uncurtained window, the straw mattresses, the dirty walls, the pungent odour of unwashed blankets.

"I am so hot!" were her first words. She removed the cloak and flung it on the nearest bed, which was William's. Then she sat down on the bench. "How can you players bear to wear such stuff? It scratches like the points of a thousand rapiers."

"Your complexion is too fine for cheap stage costumes," said Sam gallantly as he lit the candles.

Lucie's beauty emerged from the gloom, more powerful and more tender than Sam remembered. He sat beside her and gazed upon her, not caring if she saw how overwhelming was his admiration. She was wearing a square-necked damask dress of a sober colour. It was plainer than any clothes Sam had seen her in before. Over it, to Sam's slight embarrassment, she wore an apron. It was a good disguise, but something in him baulked at the sight of a noble lady in servants' clothing.

She looked earnestly into his face. "Sam, do you believe that love can overcome any obstacle? If it is true love, that is? Some people will tell you that is a ridiculous notion. But I believe it."

Sam's heart began to thump. Blood rushed to his cheeks; his body was flooded with a sensation of love both noble and passionate. Lucie's eyes reflected her words. He could not deny her. "I do, too," he said. "Of course I do."

"I knew you would! I believe that the very first time we saw each other, on the day after Christmas – half a year ago, now – something was drawing us together."

Sam smiled, and took her hand. "I thought you were the most beautiful girl I had ever seen."

"I thought you were beautiful too."

"I?" Sam was genuinely disbelieving. "I am not beautiful!"

She shook her head impatiently. "You are not a living Adonis, such as William Hughes considers himself to be. But that is not my notion of masculine beauty. Who would prefer a Greek statue to flesh and blood such as yours?" She studied him seriously. "The darkness of your eyes, Sam, is mysterious and delightful. There is a light in them which shines when you are acting, and when you are happy, but diminishes when you are not. And the way your head sits upon your shoulders, and the elegance with which you turn it – whether you are wearing a skirt or not! – makes me able to tell you from anyone else at a hundred paces."

"You may always tell me by my lack of height," said Sam ruefully. "Though I have grown a little this past year."

"You are tall enough," declared Lucie. "And your shoulder is broad and your arm is strong. *That* is what manly beauty is, in my opinion. I could not free myself from the memory of your countenance after that Christmas night. And when I saw you again on New Year's Eve I was in no doubt that I wished to know you better."

"You smiled at me," said Sam, smiling himself at the memory. "I was ready to faint, I was so surprised that a fine lady should smile at a player."

"It is my title, not my heart, that makes me a fine lady," said Lucie. "I know a kindred heart when I meet it, whatever profession its owner belongs to. Is yours my kindred heart, Sam?"

He did not hesitate. "It is."

"Shall we be together, in spite of all the difficulties?"

It was much easier to declare himself than Sam had feared. The words were from his heart, and it was easy to speak a heartfelt truth. "Lucie, I will do anything to win you for my own."

"Indeed?" she replied teasingly. "Are you after my wealth and connections?"

"Yes, of course," he replied, mock-solemnly.

She smiled. "And why else do you wish to win me, Sam?"

"You know that you are beautiful, so I do not need to tell you that. But I also admire your wit."

"My wit!" She digested this. "And what else?"

"Your fearlessness." He thought for a moment, remembering how she had held his hand as they sat among the forest of pillars under the gallery. "And your compassion. You are a rare person – one who has tried to understand what it is like for a boy to leave home at a young age and live among strangers."

Without warning, she slid her arms around his waist. "Oh, Sam! In anyone else I would suspect this to be gallantry, but from you I know it is sincere."

Sam put his arms round her. Her body felt frail in its rigid stomacher and stiff, hooped farthingale. His head was full of things he could not say, though he dearly wished to, and his heart was scarcely less crammed. He wanted to take Lucie to a far-off place, away from everyone in the world, and talk, talk, talk to her, and look into her lovely face for ever.

"Now I will tell you the reasons I have chosen you,"

she said demurely. "Are you ready?"

"Quite ready."

"You do not debase yourself in my presence, but neither do you treat me as if I am a piece of property to be handed around like a roasted goose on a plate."

"And what else?" asked Sam.

Lucie laughed. She was so close that he could feel her breath on his cheek. "For exactly that! You do not scruple to throw my words back in my face. I am not used to being mocked by young men, you know."

"I do not even notice that I do that," admitted Sam.

"Naturally you do not notice. Because you are an actor, you give of yourself freely. Every performance you do is an adventure, the outcome of which you cannot predict. How interesting your life must be!"

Sam felt as if someone had presented him with a thousand sovereigns. If he were to die tomorrow, he decided, he would not care. He had been happier here in the gloom of this attic room than he had ever been in his life. God had given him Lucie, and could now do with him what He pleased.

He could not help himself. He released her and took her face between his palms. "Lucie, may I kiss you?"

"If you do not, I shall kiss you!"

Kissing her was not like anything Sam had done before. He had kissed many actors in the course of his apprenticeship. But he had met — let alone kissed — so few real girls, he was almost overwhelmed by the softness of her lips. So powerful was the tremor that passed through his body, that for a heart-stopping moment he thought he had been attacked from behind by someone intent on knocking the wind out of him.

"Lucie … Lucie…" He caressed her face and neck, not caring where his fingers travelled. Her ears were perfect, he noticed for the first time. Her collarbone was delicately formed. He kissed the hollow in the middle of it. "Lucie…"

"Dearest," she whispered. Her face was aglow with delight and relief. "My dearest, dearest Sam, I am so happy. I never thought to find anyone like you, but God has sent you. Will you swear faithfulness to me?"

Sam bowed his head. "I swear, by Almighty God, that I will never betray you."

"Nor I you."

A church bell tolled the quarter of seven. Lucie pulled away from Sam's embrace and tidied her hair. Her cheeks had coloured; her expression was soft.

"One day, you will be mine," said Sam.

She kissed her fingers, and laid them upon his lips. Then she took the Juliet cloak from William's bed. Sam placed it round her shoulders. They went down the stairs together, and Sam watched in wonderment as she walked back to where Matty was waiting for her.

Enter Rumour

The Lord Chamberlain's Men were busier at the Globe even than they had been at the Curtain. By the time Mr Shakespeare called a meeting at his house one Sunday in September, it had been recorded by Mr Cuthbert Burbage that they had performed no fewer than ten different plays, including three new ones. The long days of summer allowed for two performances daily, and large crowds showed their loyalty to the company by their willingness to take the ferry to Southwark whenever the flag on the roof of the theatre was flying.

"We are earning enough to pay our debts for the construction of the building," announced Mr Burbage, "and some money has been put aside for new productions. We obviously cannot continue with this rate of performance in the winter, so I must ask you, gentlemen, to rise above your weariness for one month more. Then, I hope, you may be granted some rest days."

There was general approval of this. Fatigued though

they might be, the men had benefited from the move to Southwark. The company no longer had to contend with a landlord whose notions of money-making entertainments were not the same as theirs. The Globe was a fine place to work in; it had a good, large stage, and the backstage areas were far superior to those at the Curtain. The gallery was more comfortable for those who could pay twopence and threepence for their seats. Until the weather changed, the Lord Chamberlain's Men would work all the hours they could.

"Which play is it next week?" asked Mr Phillips. "John and I have a wager on *Romeo and Juliet*, which I say is due for an airing. But he says not. Who is to win, Will?"

Mr Shakespeare smiled. "John has won," he said. "It is not *Romeo*. But you will soon discover which play we *are* doing, Augustine, as I have called this meeting to do a reading of it."

Sam liked Sunday readings. There were never enough full scripts to go round, so Sam would usually only be given a cue script, his own lines with their cues scrawled above them. While the senior men were arguing over entrances and exits and moves, Sam could have a rest and dream.

"Next week," continued Mr Shakespeare, "we shall do several performances of *The First Part of King Henry the Fourth* and *The Second Part of King Henry the Fourth*." From a cupboard in the corner of the room he produced a pile of dog-eared papers. "We shall perform the two Henrys on alternate afternoons throughout the week, in preparation for next Friday's performance of a new play, which is a sequel to the other two," he explained as he distributed the papers. "Its title, as I probably do not need to inform you, is *King Henry the Fifth*. For now, let us read through the older plays. Then, after supper, I invite you to embark upon a first reading of the new one."

Sam was interested. The two plays about King Henry the Fourth, the highly respected ancestor of Queen Elizabeth, had always been popular. Playgoers loved them for their variety, since they contained every kind of character Mr Shakespeare's imagination could produce. But they were hard work for the company. Scenes of tavern low life alternated with serious discussions between the king and his son, Prince Henry. Clowns kept the crowd amused, and there was plenty of music, fighting and royal spectacle. All but the most senior players had to double, or even treble. Energetic young Nathan Field was put to good use as a drawer who served the beer, a groom, a servant and a reluctant army recruit as well as playing his most important part, Falstaff's page.

And then there was Falstaff himself. Mr Kempe had made the part of this red-faced, large-bellied, hard-drinking, wench-loving friend to Prince Henry entirely his own. He could portray Sir John Falstaff as both funny and pathetic, doomed to rejection by Prince Henry once the crown was on the young prince's head. However many times Sam acted in the plays he could not understand how this double effect was achieved. To have the crowd screaming with laughter one moment, and in anxious silence, even tears, the next, seemed impossible. Yet Sam had seen Mr Kempe do it time and again, as affectingly as if it were the only performance he would ever do in his life.

Mr Heminges and Mr Pope were arguing with Mr Shakespeare about doubling, insisting that they did not have long enough to change their costumes.

"Gentlemen, we established long ago that twenty-seven lines is sufficient," Mr Shakespeare told them wearily. "Surely, if you were able to change in time last year, then you will be able to do so now."

"We had more money last year, Will, and could hire more men," said Mr Pope. "Could you not cut out some characters?"

"No, Tom, the plays are too well known for that," said Mr Heminges.

"But we have not the money for more men," insisted Mr Pope, who took his position as a part-owner of the Globe very seriously. "Our receipts for these first three months might be good, but they are not so good that we can afford to be profligate with our funds. Giles Allen will be on our backs like a vulture at the first hint that we have fallen into worse debt, or that the Globe is a failure."

"The Globe is not a failure!" Mr Shakespeare looked around the assembled company. "Men of the Lord Chamberlain's patronage, are you willing to play these fifty parts, though you number only fifteen?" He did not wait for the answer. "Of course you are!"

He turned sympathetically to Mr Heminges, who was shaking his head. "Tom is right, John," he said. "We have not the money. It is fortuitous that we have today's reading to reallocate parts and work out doubling, and I value your help in this." His eye then fell on the apprentices in the window recess. "You, Nathan my lad, will have to play even more parts than usual, and you, Sam Gilburne…"

Sam, who had been only half listening, brought himself back from an examination of the translucent skin of Lucie's neck, against which her jewelled earrings lay like treasure displayed upon finest silk. "I, sir?"

"You will play Travers as usual," said Mr Shakespeare, "and one of the recruits. But you must also take the part of Rumour, and wear the costume painted full of tongues." He consulted the script of *The Second Part*. "You will be able to make the change into Travers's clothes, as there are over thirty lines before his entrance. Do you think you are ready to take on the challenge of opening a play?"

Sam nodded. "Yes, sir. Thank you, sir." It was not done in actors' society to betray too much enthusiasm at the prospect of a superior part. But his heart swelled with pride at the thought that Mr Shakespeare trusted him to arrest the attention of the still-settling audience.

"By the way, where is Master Kempe today?" asked Mr Phillips in his languid way. "In church? Surely not!"

During the short silence that followed, Sam saw Mr Heminges and Mr Pope exchange looks. "Will," said Mr Heminges, "we cannot have a full company reading without Sir John Falstaff."

Mr Shakespeare remained unperturbed, looking at no one. "I am unconcerned at Mr Kempe's absence from the readings of the older plays. He knows his lines and entrances well enough."

"So do we all," said Mr Pope quietly. "But we are here."

"Mr Kempe will join us later, for the reading of the new play," said Mr Shakespeare.

No one spoke. Gazing at the unpromising view from Mr Shakespeare's window, which was of the windows on the other side of the street, Sam recollected that it was a long time since he had seen Mr Kempe, on stage or off it. Parts that Mr Kempe had been used to playing had lately been taken by Robert Armin, whose skilful comedy was making him increasingly popular with the younger element of the crowd. Sam glanced around the room. Robert Armin was not present either, though as Mr Heminges had pointed out, this was a full company reading.

"Now, shall we begin *The First Part*?" asked Mr Shakespeare. "I believe the king has the first lines."

He stood up and began to read them. John Heminges said no more on the subject of Mr Kempe, and the afternoon wore on with its usual mixture of speed and tedium. Sam, who felt very weary, spoke little except for his lines. But after they had finished the first two plays, and Mr Shakespeare's housekeeper had supplied the men with ale and cold beef, Sam's eagerness to hear the new play was as keen as anyone else's.

During the familiar arguments over the allocation of roles, his eagerness subsided into resignation. It was clear that his newly bestowed status as Rumour in *The Second Part of King Henry the Fourth* was not to be the first of many such promotions.

"William, you are the Hostess again, and Sam, you

be Pistol," said Mr Shakespeare. "And you can both pronounce French words, can you not?"

"Aye, sir," said William, "but I am better at it than Sam."

"That matters not," said Mr Shakespeare. "I am more interested in your golden hair, William, for the part of Princess Katharine of France. Sam, I hardly need tell you that, since you have the look of a country-bred girl, you are Alice, the Princess's waiting-woman."

"Thank you, sir," murmured Sam, ignoring the laughter inevitably discharged by his fellow actors. Mr Shakespeare, ignoring it too, announced that he would take the part of the Chorus himself. And he began to read the opening speech of *King Henry the Fifth*.

Gooseflesh crept over Sam's skin. In thrilling words the Chorus called for the inspiration to make the theatre into the kingdom of England, and the actors into princes and kings. Best of all, the speech paid homage to the theatre which had risen out of the ingenuity of the company itself. It was in "this wooden O" that the re-enactment of history would be performed, with the help, the Chorus pleaded, of the audience's imagination.

Sam could hear in Mr Shakespeare's voice his pride in the Globe and in the men who performed within it. Feeling proud too, he listened to the other actors read their parts. Things went on exactly as they always did with a first reading: a few lines, a halt, a discussion, another few lines, a change, a reinstatement, another few lines. But then, just as Sam was preparing to say his own first words, things stopped being the way they always were.

"'Enter Sir John Falstaff, Hostess, and Pistol,'" read Mr Burbage from the script. "That is Mr Kempe, William Hughes and Sam Gilburne."

"Mr Kempe is still not here," said William.

Everyone looked at Mr Shakespeare, who spread his hands with an expression more of sorrow than irritation. His dark eyes looked very dark.

"We cannot read the scene without Falstaff, Will," observed Mr Burbage wearily, consulting the script. "We had better go on to the next one. Are you ready, gentlemen?"

"Do not trouble yourselves." Mr Shakespeare's patience, usually so difficult to try, had evidently been broken. He stood up. "William Hughes and Sam Gilburne, you will read the scene without Mr Kempe."

Frowning, he seized the page from Mr Burbage's hand and went to his writing table. He took pen and ink and scribbled for some minutes. Then he handed the paper to William. "There, Master Hughes."

There was silence as William's eyes skimmed the new scene. It was Mr Phillips who found his voice first, but he spoke for all the others. "For God's sake, man, you cannot cast *Hughes* as Falstaff! 'Twill make a laughing stock of the company! I beg you to reconsider!"

Mr Shakespeare looked into his face. "It is *you* that needs to reconsider, Augustine. Do you think I am so consumed with the desire for vengeance that I will ruin my play in order to make Mr Kempe's conduct plain before the world? No, William Hughes is not to play Falstaff. No one is. I have killed Falstaff off."

William looked up from the script, his eyes alight. "He has, masters. Sir John Falstaff is not in the scene at all, and the Hostess is to say he is gravely ill. Then, the next time she comes in…" He turned the page over and read on. "…she is to say Falstaff is dead."

"Falstaff *is* dead," said Mr Shakespeare with finality. "At least in this play. The next time we do the two *King Henry the Fourth* plays, Mr Armin can play him. Mr Kempe has left the company by mutual consent."

"Mutual consent in his absence?" returned Mr Heminges, who was ever concerned for the welfare of company members. "How can that be?"

"John, this matter is closed," insisted Mr Shakespeare. He regarded the subdued faces of Mr Heminges, Mr Burbage, Mr Phillips and Mr Pope. Then he stood a moment, looking at nothing, stroking his beard with the feather end of the pen. "The services of Mr Kempe are no longer required. That is all I have to say."

He tucked the quill inside his doublet. Sam noticed that his hands were shaking. "Now, William Hughes," he said, "read the Hostess. Tell us Falstaff is dead." When William hesitated, Mr Shakespeare slapped the table impatiently. "Read it, I say!"

William read it.

The nervousness Sam had been hiding all morning had begun to strangle him. How was he going to produce the volume of voice needed to quiet the crowd? In ten minutes he would have to do it. Supposing he opened his mouth and no sound came out? Would Mr

Shakespeare ever give him a decent part again? The inevitable answer to this question made him feel worse.

"Here it is," said William, holding the Rumour costume at arm's length. "Phaw!"

"All our costumes stink, William," observed Sam quietly.

"Not as bad as this one. Here it comes. Hold your breath."

He helped Sam pull the costume over his head. The canvas tunic, stiffened by the thickly painted tongues, was indeed smelly. And it was uncomfortable. The close-fitting hat that went with it, also painted with curling lips and tongues, hid Sam's hair completely. He held the white mask before his face and regarded himself in the glass. He looked malevolent, to be sure, as Rumour should. But the costume also made him an anonymous, non-human character, forcing him to leave his real self outside it like the accomplished actor he was striving to become.

He peeped through the spyhole in the door. In a true representation of its name, the Globe was alive with every possible permutation of humanity. Sam loved to see it like this. The continuing popularity of the two Henrys was evident in the noise, the heat and the stench of two thousand bodies packed into a confined space on a warm September afternoon. He had never seen so many heads in the pit below the stage before, not even for that memorable opening performance of *Julius Caesar*. The galleries too were crowded with onlookers. Everyone was talking, or eating, or drinking, or all three. And it was Sam's responsibility to silence them.

"Go on, Sam!" called Nathan, who had received Mr Shakespeare's signal.

No one took much notice of Sam as he took up his position at the front of the stage. No one laughed at his strange costume. The shouted conversations continued. He opened his mouth to say his first line as loudly as he could, but then he closed it again. A picture had come to him of Mr Shakespeare, dressed to play King Henry the Fourth in his grey wig and beard, his eye pressed so close to the spyhole that his crown was knocked sideways, watching what young Sam Gilburne was going to do.

Sam did not speak. He stood in the middle of the stage for a count of ten, and he walked to one corner of the apron that jutted out into the yard where the groundlings stood. Then he walked to the other corner, all the while fixing his eyes upon those closest to him. Gradually, they began to silence their neighbours, who began to silence theirs. The din decreased to a murmur, and then a few isolated voices, and then no more than the shuffling of feet and the cries of infants. Two thousand expectant faces turned to Sam. His heart bulging, he spread his arms, threw back his head and pleaded, "'Open your ears; for which of you will stop the vent of hearing when loud Rumour speaks?'"

They *did* open their ears, and he did not even have to be "loud" Rumour. He spoke at his usual actor's volume, and even stage-whispered some lines. Relieved that he had completed this lonely, nerve-wracking task, he realized as he left the stage that sweat was soaking his clothes.

Off stage, the usual bustle met him. He tore off Rumour's hat and mask, and William pulled the tongue-painted tunic over Sam's head. There were only thirty lines before his next entrance. Sam wiped his drenched face and hair, put on Travers's hat, adjusted Travers's doublet and made haste once more for the stage in time to hear Mr Pope say, "'Now, Travers, what good tidings come with you?'"

Every fibre of his body was stretched as tight as a lute string. The usual surge of excitement that accompanied every performance swept over him tenfold as he said Travers's lines. Below him the groundlings swayed in a solid mass, this way and that as they followed the action. From the galleries came murmured approval as the familiar story of the rebellion against King Henry unfolded. All around, the spell of the drama cast itself upon Sam as well as on any member of the audience. Being an actor, possessed of this power, was his destiny and his desire. He was indeed bewitched.

The play went on, as unstoppable once it had been set in motion as a bolting horse. It was not until much later, when the yard lay in shadow, that Sam heard his name called. Mr Shakespeare was sitting on the front bench of the lowest gallery. Sam had been about to leave the theatre, but he put down his pack and stood in front of his master. He felt like a felon on trial at the Assizes. "Yes, sir?"

"You know what I am going to say, do you not, Master Sam?"

"No, sir, I do not."

"Do you expect praise?"

"I expect nothing, sir."

Mr Shakespeare leaned forward, resting his elbows on the rail and eyeing Sam keenly. Sam looked at the floor.

"Sam Gilburne, you have today achieved something rich and strange."

Sam waited, saying nothing.

"You are nearer manhood than you were yesterday, and not only because of the passage of twenty-four hours."

Sam swallowed. "Indeed, sir?"

"Yes, indeed. Do you think you are a good actor, Sam?"

He could not immediately answer. Something – or everything, perhaps – had become clear. He was a good actor, and would be a better one. More important, there was nothing in the world he would rather do than acting. He swallowed again, and spoke. "I think I have the makings of one, when I work hard, sir."

"And when do you *not* work hard?"

Sam could not very well reply. Mr Shakespeare sighed, rose, and donned his hat. "I pray you, Sam Gilburne, do not turn your hand to playwriting, as young Nathan is always saying he will do some day. You see, I do not fear Nathan's talent, but God knows I fear yours."

Sam's success as Rumour did not result in any obvious glory. Things did not happen like that in the Lord Chamberlain's Men. One day you were important, the next you were an apprentice again, put on the earth to be abused by your seniors and mocked by your peers. On Friday, with the cheers that followed the first performance of *King Henry the Fifth* still sounding in his memory, and fatigued beyond expression, Sam sat down in the last light of the September evening to write to Lucie.

Shoredich, 28 September 1599

Dearest Lucie,

I trust this letter finds you well. I am of good cheer, but very tired. This week I acted Rumour in The Second Part of King Henry the Fourth. *I had to enter alone and command the attention of all. My costume is surely one of the strangest I have ever worn – a tunic made of material far rougher than the Juliet cloak, and painted full of tongues. It was very hot and smelled to heaven. But Mr Shakespeare praised my efforts.*

Today we performed for the first time a new play, King Henry the Fifth, *in which Mr Shakespeare pays homage to your illustrious uncle and his mission in Ireland. He calls him "the general of our gracious empress" and imagines the people of London turning out in their thousands to welcome him home, whenever he has succeeded in quelling the Irish rebellion. I do not need to describe the din the audience made when they heard this! There is no denying that Lord Essex is their greatest hero.*

It is now three months since we met, my most dear Lucie, and I cannot wait any longer to see you. I wish you could see me play Rumour, and hear the crowd cheering the lines about your uncle. The three Henry plays will be performed next week too. Might you prevail upon your aunts to bring you to the Globe, trick them in some way and meet me under the gallery as you did after King Richard the Second *at the Curtain?*

I hope with all my heart that you are in good health, and I await your reply with impatience and inexpressible love. I will bid you good morrow now. Write to me soon.

All my love,
  Sam

He sealed the letter and pondered upon the question of how to get it to Lucie. Today was Friday. After next week the Henrys would be replaced by comedies. If Lucie were to see him as Rumour – and Sam greatly desired that she should – he had no time to await a letter brought by Matty, and then send his own letter back with her. No, he must go to Essex House itself, and he must go this very evening.

He remembered that Matty had told him not to do this. But he reasoned that if he went to the back entrance, and asked to see Matty in person, it could do no harm. Messengers must arrive constantly at such a place, even in the evening. He grinned as he put on his cap. It would be very entertaining to see the expression on Matty's face. And, if his star was in the right part of the heavens, Sam might even spy Lucie at an upstairs window, waving to him.

Essex House was on the Strand. As its name indicated, this street ran alongside the river at a part where a wide beach was exposed at low tide. Its aspect was open and its location close to Westminster and Whitehall, so it had become the residence of many aristocratic servants of the queen. Sam, needless to say, had never set foot there before.

On that mild September night when he made his way from the Blackfriars ferry landing, his precious letter hidden inside his shirt, the tide was high. The river water sucked and gurgled around the pales of the boat moorings along the Strand, the sound of the debris floating on its surface noticeable in the still air. Sam pulled his cap low over his eyes and hurried along, trying to look like an apprentice on legitimate business. He wished he had thought to bring a pack or a box, but it was too late now.

He did not know the exact location of Essex House, so all he could do was inspect each building in the hope that it would display the coat of arms of its occupant. He knew Lord Essex's crest well enough, but he had no fear of meeting the man himself. Lord Essex, as the Chorus in *King Henry the Fifth* had proclaimed that very afternoon, was still in Ireland.

Above the carved portal of a house near the Westminster end of the street, he saw the Essex arms. He could not be mistaken. The house stood square and solid in a garden reaching to the riverside, divided from the road by a shoulder-high wall. To the side there was an alley, with a gate in the wall which Sam hoped led to the servants' entrance.

There was no one about. The busy thoroughfares of Blackfriars, Shoreditch and Southwark might as well be a hundred miles away. There were no taverns here, no places of public gathering. There was not even a public ferry. The houses enjoyed a private aspect, and their residents would hire boatmen to row them up and down the river. When Lucie ventured out in the street she did not have to pick her way in her dainty shoes through filth such as Sam encountered every day. A coach would await her outside the door, and she would be handed into it by a page. If Mr Shakespeare decided never to employ Sam as a hired man, he mused as he opened the little gate in the wall, perhaps he could get employment as a page in this house, and see Lucie every day.

On the other side of the gate a path led through the garden to a divided door, the top half of which was open to the late summer air. Beyond it stretched a dark passageway. He knocked loudly. "Is Mistress Matty at home?" he called.

A door at the other end of the passageway opened. But it was not Matty who appeared. It was, to his astonishment, Lucie herself.

Sam's legs weakened. His star *was* in the right part of the heavens. He leaned on the doorframe, looking at Lucie in as uncouth a manner as any ruffian who might catch sight of her in the street. He could not stop himself. She looked more beautiful even than he remembered. She looked like an angel, though a youthful one. Perhaps a cherub. Or were both angels and cherubs boys? His thoughts in disarray, he could not speak.

She did not speak either. There was a shining in her eyes that Sam realized, suddenly, was tears. "What is it?" he asked her.

The tears splashed over her eyelids. Her shoulders began to shake. "You must go away from here. You should not have come. It is too dangerous."

"Why? No one has seen us."

"No, but the risk is too great."

"I do not understand."

"Sam." She laid her hand on his arm. "My Lord Essex is no longer in Ireland. He has deserted his post. He and Lord Southampton, and a few others, have returned."

Sam felt as if an arrow had hit him in the chest. He actually reeled, and had to take a step backwards to steady himself. "Deserted! But that is punishable by… "

Lucie's tears made it impossible for him to go on. He put his arms around her and she sobbed quietly for a few moments. Then she raised her head. "There is worse," she said wretchedly. "This morning, straight from his arrival, he rode to the queen's palace at Nonsuch and burst into the royal bedchamber unannounced. Oh, Sam! The queen did not even have her wig on!"

She could not continue. Sam could hardly breathe. To arrive in the queen's presence unbidden was very questionable behaviour at the best of times. But to burst into her *bedchamber*, bearing such news as Lord Essex had to unburden himself of! Desertion and abandonment of his troops in Ireland were bad enough, but to increase the fury of the queen by such means was almost beyond belief. The man had clearly gone mad.

"Lucie … how do you know this?"

"A letter was brought to my Lady Rich an hour ago. Fearful that the news might bring a fever upon Lady Essex – she was delivered of her child only last week – my Aunt Penelope stayed with her in her chamber after she had read the letter to us. I went to my room, and looked out of the window, and saw you. I watched you wending your way up the street, peering at every house. I knew you were looking for me, like a knight coming to rescue a damsel, and how beloved that made me feel!"

"You *are* beloved, Lucie."

Again she collapsed against him. He tried to muster his wits. "Where is Lord Essex now?"

"Oh, do not fear! He is not in the house. He has been taken to York House, further upriver from here. He is under arrest, Sam, though I suppose we should be thankful he has not been imprisoned in the Tower."

Sam did not know what to do. Any attempt to soothe Lucie seemed insulting, given the enormity of the event. "I will not come to the house again if you do not wish it," he said, feeling foolish, "but I came this evening to bring you this letter."

She took the letter, crumpled by their embrace. She read it quickly. Then she looked into Sam's face. "I cannot attend the Globe, nor indeed go anywhere in peace any more. I am tainted by Lord Essex's disgrace." She touched his cheek tenderly. "I must remember your beautiful face, for it may be a long time before I see it again. And you had better look to the fortunes of the Lord Chamberlain's Men. They have long enjoyed the friendship of Lord Essex and Lord Southampton. Not I, nor my aunts, nor Mr Shakespeare, nor anyone known to have associated with Lord Essex's circle, is safe from the queen's wrath."

Sam took her hand and drew it to his lips. When he had kissed it he held it against his cheek, trying to imprint her touch and her scent upon his memory.

"Lord Essex has gone too far this time, Sam," she said, her voice shaking. "I fear he may have hastened his fall. But let us pray to God that he will not take all of us down with him."

It was rumoured that the queen planned to hang, draw and quarter Lord Essex for his unseemly interruption of her toilette. It was rumoured that both he and Lord Southampton were to be tried immediately for treason, before the week was out. It was rumoured that the younger man, though spared the agonizing death which awaited Lord Essex, would be beheaded. It was even rumoured that the queen would make an exception to her usual rule, and watch both executions personally. Londoners, as easily swayed as the Romans in *Julius Caesar*, were not in the mood to be kind.

Sam reflected sourly that Rumour was no character in a play. It was real, and it was as active in the court of Queen Elizabeth the First as it had ever been in that of King Henry the Fourth. Each morning brought new stories, and each evening saw them exposed as no more than the tongue-wagging of sensationalists. People were as ready with their condemnation as they had ever been with their adoration. The senior members of the Lord Chamberlain's Men, though erstwhile supporters of Lord Essex, understood the danger in remaining publicly so, and tightened their lips. Sam did not know, and could not ask, what their private opinions were.

One story did turn out to be true. Upon the orders of Sir Robert Cecil, the Queen's Secretary of State, Essex House had been put under armed guard. Cecil could not imprison Lord Essex's relatives, since they had not been accused of anything, but he could use his influence to persuade the queen to curtail their freedom. No one, even Lady Essex herself, could leave or enter without being searched and followed. Not only was it impossible for Lucie to attend the Globe, but her correspondence with Sam was extinguished.

Longing, followed by immediate dismissal of that longing, rushed over Sam as soon as he had taken his bow after each performance. It filled the space where his concentration on the play had been. He longed to protect Lucie from any possible harm that might come to her, all her life. He longed to touch the fine, velvety skin he knew he would encounter under the outer armour of clothing ladies wore – clothing designed, he was sure, to frustrate exactly such desires.

But to do that, to make her entirely his own as Romeo had made Juliet his own, he would have to climb obstacles so high that even a playwright would not dare to invent them. And Lord Essex's behaviour had only made them higher. Now, in this atmosphere of suspicion, where even the most innocent action could be interpreted as treasonable, merely to write a letter to Lucie might cost Sam his freedom, or his life. The possibility of seeing her again, holding her in his arms, telling her he loved her, had become so utterly, stupidly remote, it hurt his brain even to think about it.

Although he told himself to remain calm, and that the situation could not last for ever, it was hard to be optimistic. Even if she were freed, and remained in

London instead of returning to the safety of Northumberland, how could he ever achieve what he dreamed of? Titled ladies did not marry players. And it mattered little that Lucie was quite different from an ordinary titled lady. Her father would never give his consent.

In order to have the smallest chance of succeeding, Sam would have to give up the life he loved and take on a profession suitable for a gentleman. Tears pricked his eyes whenever the thought came to him, unbeckoned, in the middle of restless nights or warm, wearisome days: in order to win Lucie, he must lose everything else.

The Dilemma

That October was the warmest England had known for many years. The Lord Chamberlain's Men continued to perform ten or eleven times a week, six days out of seven, during sunny afternoons and balmy evenings. *King Henry the Fifth* proved to be as popular as the two previous Henrys. There was talk among the men of presenting it at court, but as the company made to leave the theatre after the play's final performance of the season, Mr Burbage expressed doubts.

"I fear that in the present climate (and I am not referring to the weather, gentlemen), even the patriotic theme of *King Henry the Fifth*, and the artistic merit of the play, are not enough to secure the honour of an invitation to court."

"Artistic merit!" snorted Mr Shakespeare. "Let us hope there will be some left after all the cuts I will have to make. We can no longer mention Lord Essex's triumphant return from Ireland, for a start."

"That is, unfortunately, true," agreed Mr Burbage.

"However, Lord Essex is not come to trial yet. Let us hope for a happy outcome."

Despite the necessary withdrawal of Lord Southampton's patronage, the sharers reported high takings, and Mr Shakespeare announced that at last the men could have a few days' rest. After Saturday's performances, they would not be required until Thursday afternoon, for *Julius Caesar*.

Sam and Robert were in no hurry to go back to the chamber in Shoreditch they now shared with Nathan Field. So they accompanied William, who, as a hired man, no longer had to answer to anyone for his whereabouts or his company, back to the lodgings he had recently taken in Southwark. They sauntered between ditches as dry as they ever could be. Although it was past seven o'clock, the air was barely tinged with the chill of autumn. It was glorious weather, and the three friends had been granted four consecutive days off. Sam knew he should be rejoicing, yet his chest felt tight. When they reached William's room, which was at the top of a house free from a gossiping landlady and interested neighbours, he sat on the window seat and wondered if Lucie were watching this same summer sky and thinking about him.

"Four days of freedom!" William knelt beside Sam and opened the casement upon the golden evening. "Liquor, wenches, food and sleep, blessed sleep! That is what I call freedom!"

"And I," agreed Robert. "But I will wager that Master Sam here has different ideas…"

He gave Sam a lecherous glance, which looked so incongruous on Robert's youthful features that Sam almost laughed. "No, Robert," he said, "you are quite wrong. There is no possibility of a meeting. I cannot even correspond with her, now that Essex House is under guard."

Robert's face rearranged itself into its usual wide-eyed expression. "Not at all?"

"No, not at all," explained Sam. He looked around nervously. William pulled the window closed. Nevertheless, Sam lowered his voice. "A watch is kept on the house day and night. Matty, the maidservant, would be searched, and it would be discovered that Lord Essex's niece is corresponding with a player in the Lord Chamberlain's Men. Think, Robert. Her Majesty knows that Lord Essex is one of our most valued friends. If he *were* planning anything, what better way could be found to recruit supporters than through an innocent-seeming correspondence between Lucie and me?"

Robert and William were silent. Then Robert said, "But it *is* innocent, Sam, is it not?"

"Oh, Robert!" Sam patted his friend's shoulder, amused by Robert's lack of guile, but also disturbed by the fear on his face. "Of course it is, but Sir Robert Cecil and the queen's other advisors do not know that. I would find myself in the Tower before you could eat a quarter of a pound of cheese, and you know how short a time that is!"

Robert did not look very reassured, but he nodded. "Very well, Sam. William and I have not breathed a word of your … er … friendship with this lady, and we shall not, shall we, William? We do not wish to see you thrown into the Tower."

"Indeed," added William. "If Sam were imprisoned, or even executed, who would be Hero to my Beatrice? I refuse to play opposite that piping Nathan Field!"

Robert looked incredulous at this flippancy, but Sam welcomed it. William's remark exposed, and therefore weakened, the fear they all felt.

"What shall *you* do with your four days of rest, Robert?" asked Sam. "While William is drinking, wenching and sleeping?"

"I must go to visit my mother. I have not seen her for almost a year," said Robert resignedly.

"She is a widow, is she not?" asked Sam.

"Aye, my father has been dead these seven years. And she does not know about my 'accident' at the theatre. When she sees my scarred face, I know not what she will do. I only hope she allows me to come back on Thursday! She cried so much when I first came to London I thought she would never stop. And she kept saying what a vast city it was, and wondering how I would find my way in it."

Sam nodded, remembering his own introduction to London, when he had stood with his father in the prow of the boat that had brought them round the Kent coast from Eastbourne. It had been an autumn evening not unlike this one, clear and still. His father had taken a calm leave of his thirteen-year-old son, shaking him by the hand and entreating him to behave like a gentleman. It was four years ago, but it seemed longer.

"I shall follow your example, Robert," he said, making the decision almost as he spoke. "The Bailiff will surely have no objection to granting a licence for a poor player to return to his family for a few days. I shall leave at daybreak on Sunday, and hope for a fair wind. I too have not been home for more than a year. Nearer two, indeed."

What would his parents think of him? Would his brothers and sisters still run to meet him on the Eastbourne road, or had they outgrown such childish ways? He had got taller and bigger, and his hair had darkened, so that even in two years he looked different. Would they approve of the transformation? And would his father consider his manners to be those of a gentleman, as he had wished?

"I envy you," said William. "Three days in the fresh air! If only a certain lady were there with you!"

At these words, Sam's senses sharpened. The scent of the hay his father and brothers would at this moment be cutting wafted into his imagination. A lass and her swain, and a haystack, as the song he had sung for Mr Shakespeare went…

"That is impossible, William," he said. "We are not to have the pleasure of her company for a long time. At present only her servants may see her at close quarters."

"Hah!" cried William. "I have often observed how a lowly servant has more opportunities in one day to be near a fine lady than we actors have in a lifetime. And yet our status is well above that of a servant!"

"Yours may be," Sam replied, "but mine is still that of an apprentice, and I well remember you saying that there is no difference between an apprentice and a serving wench, apart from the obvious one."

"True. Yet you have been closer to the lady than any

of her servants." He looked carefully at Sam. Still fearful, still aware of the folly of unguarded discussion, he did not speak her name. "And you will be again, if there is any justice in the world."

Sam returned his friend's look. "I thank you from my heart, William."

"Robert and I shall dance at your wedding yet," said William, opening the window again.

The fields looked smaller than Sam remembered them. On his last visit to the farm it had been a wet winter, and during his two-day visit he had barely ventured out of doors. But today the autumn sun shone on the bent backs of the workers – Sam himself, his brothers Edward and Francis, his sister Clarice, his mother, his father and three hands employed for the harvesting.

Little Anne was yet too young to reap or stack, but she was usefully engaged in gathering loose stalks from the stubble and putting them into nosebags to be given to the horses that pulled the haycart. And if she spent less time gleaning than climbing on and off the cart and talking to the horses, no one minded. This year's crop had grown well. There had been sufficient rain and sunshine, and on Sam's first evening his father had remarked at supper that the weather looked set fair for another week at least.

"'Tis the very best time of year for you to visit, Sam," he had observed. "When another pair of hands is most useful."

"Mr Shakespeare seems to understand the ways of country folk," Sam's mother had added.

"Mr Shakespeare understands many things," Sam

had informed them with pride. "He is a country man himself. His home is in Warwickshire, a place called Stratford. He is not a Londoner by birth. And did you know he has a daughter exactly of Clarice's age?"

Sam was not used to farm work. Long before it was time to rest he found his back aching beyond endurance, and his hands lacerated by stalks and blistered by the handle of the scythe. He realized ruefully that he needed his leather gloves, but looking around, he saw that no one else, even Clarice, wore gloves. In a mere four years he had become a city-dwelling milksop – quite lily-livered, as Mr Shakespeare would say. The pair of hands his father had so appreciated was not very useful after all.

He sat down in the shade of an oak tree, one of a line that marked the boundary of his father's land. Beyond the valley, the green and golden fields stretched up the hill. Sam knew that beyond it lay the twinkling blue stripe of the sea. He resolved to go down to the shore one evening before he went back to London, and breathe that salty air again.

The beauty of Sussex, so easily buried by the unrelenting work of his city life, rose to the surface again. Thinking about it made him think of that other beautiful presence, sitting with her embroidery in the garden of Essex House, or at her window overlooking the river. Perhaps she wrote him letters she could not send. Perhaps she stored them in a locked box, for him to read when circumstances allowed. If they ever did.

Surrounded by the countryside's autumn glory, he felt despondent. The stakes Lord Essex and his friends played were high. The net which would inevitably close around them was too strong. Sir Robert Cecil had influential friends and was highly favoured by the queen. Even the public popularity on which Lord Essex and Lord Southampton had so long depended could not now be guaranteed. Everyone at court was too fearful for their own skin, too influenced by gossip, too willing to renounce former admiration for the disgraced men.

According to Mr Burbage, Lord Essex had been arrested under the charge of "great and high contempts and points of misgovernance". Contempt for the queen's privacy might be added to the contempt for her authority that had been laid at Lord Essex's door. And as for misgovernance – the earl's conduct in Ireland was a clear indication of that. Entering into a truce with the Irish rebels' leader rather than subduing them was one thing, but deserting his men and fleeing back to England with Lord Southampton would be seen by the queen as a hair's breadth away from treason.

His trial would be held next summer, it was said. Eight or nine months might pass before Sam could even catch a glimpse of Lucie, unless the guard on Essex House were lifted. And what if the trial went against Lord Essex?

"Are you sleeping, Sam?"

It was Clarice. Now a well-grown girl of fifteen, she had approached across the field while he was deep in thought. She carried bread and bacon, and a flagon of beer. "Shall you and I eat our dinner here? Or do you want me to go away?"

"Of course I do not want you to go away," said Sam,

taking the provisions from her and setting them down by the tree. "I have had scarcely a moment to speak to you since I arrived, and I dare not go back to London without hearing all you have to tell me."

"And telling me something of your life too?" asked Clarice.

The setting of her brown eyes, Sam noticed, was reminiscent of her trusting, tender childhood expression. Yet it was different. The tenderness was still there, but the trust was harder to discern. He watched her kneel down and lay out the food, her half-sleeves revealing the muscles in her arms. Over her dress she wore an apron of a design not unlike the one Lucie had worn that day in Sam's room. Her hair, smoothed away from a central parting into a knitted snood, was also reminiscent of Lucie's. His sister, he concluded, was not as beautiful as a lady whose hands had never touched a scythe, and whose complexion never saw the sun. But she had her own beauty, and one day some farmer's son would come and claim her, as Sam so longed to claim Lucie.

"What do you wish to know?" he asked her.

"I wish to know why you have changed so."

Sam took his knife from his pocket and wiped it on his breeches. He cut a slice of bacon for himself and one for Clarice, and handed her a piece of the bread. "I am changed because I am older, that is all, child."

"I am not a child. But it is because you think I am a child that you will not tell me the true reason you have changed."

Sam stared at her. "What do you mean?"

"When you first came back from London, two years

ago," she explained, "you told us about everything that you had done, from the moment you woke up until the moment you went to sleep, and you made humorous observations on it all. Do you not remember how Mother laughed to see you imitate Mistress Corrie? But this time you are almost silent. You have told us which plays you have been in, and that Mr Shakespeare praised your work, and that sort of thing. But you have told us neither what you do when you are not on stage, nor what you are thinking, or hoping, or dreaming about. Edward and Francis are as disappointed as I am. It is as if we have lost another of our brothers."

Sam swallowed his mouthful, his brain working quickly. "Clarice, I am much more responsible now," he said. "When I used to chatter on as you describe, I was a young boy with nothing to be concerned about. I could laugh at everyone. But now I carry cares upon my shoulders like the rest of the company. I work hard all the time. Nothing happens to me that would entertain you or the family."

He took another bite. But his sister did not begin her meal. She sat back on her heels, with her bread and bacon in her apron and her knife in her hand, watching him with suspicious eyes. "I do not believe you, Sam Gilburne," she said deliberately. "I think you are involved with something that would break our parents' hearts if they knew about it, so you will not speak unless you betray it."

Surprise at her perception closed Sam's throat. His food filled his mouth and rendered him dumb.

"Please, tell me, my dearest Sam," implored Clarice. "If you are in trouble, I cannot bear to think of you carrying the burden alone. Share it with me. I may be able to help you. And I will never tell Mother and Father, I swear."

Sam still did not speak. He looked away from her, concentrating on swallowing. Her expression disturbed him – pleading, anxious, hoping to regain trust in a brother who had not proved trustworthy. He *was* in trouble, though not of the kind she imagined. He was not in debt or accused of a crime; he had not got a wench with child or taken a foolhardy wager. But he was in danger of bringing ruin, or possibly even worse, upon those who gave him his livelihood, the Lord Chamberlain's Men. And all for what? For a young girl not much different in essentials from Clarice herself.

"I do not carry the burden alone," he said at last. "But those who know of it are friends."

"William and Robert? And you trust them to keep your secret?"

"I do."

His sister spoke softly. Her face was troubled, but full of compassion. "Who is she, Sam?"

Sam thought for a moment. Confession was tempting, but he resisted. "I cannot tell you."

"Then why did you tell William and Robert?"

"I did not. They found out. It was beyond my control."

"They saw you with her? Oh, Sam! If you were trying to keep her a secret, how could you be so careless? What if they get drunk while you are away, and speak aloud when they should not, to someone who should not hear?"

Sam put down his knife. He did not want to eat any more. What had William promised would fill up these four free days? Drinking, and not remembering anything about it afterwards, of course. This was plain enough for a mere girl, a fifteen-year-old who did not even know the secret herself, to see. Leaning against the tree trunk, he reached for the flagon and took a draught of the weak, everyday beer brewed by his mother. He wished for something stronger.

But he remained Clarice's older brother, and must behave accordingly. "My dear Clarice," he said. He took another draught. "I know what I am doing. And I swear to you now that one day you will welcome as your sister one of the most beautiful and accomplished ladies in the kingdom. I must believe that, or misery will overcome me. But for now, I cannot share her identity with you."

The words came from his heart. Clarice saw this, and embraced him. "I shall look forward to that day, Sam. And if Tom were here, he would too. He loved you every bit as dearly as I do, you know."

It was Sam's last evening. Although the weather had still not broken, darkness fell earlier each day, and the tawny light of autumn lay across the valley. The farmhouse kitchen was so warm that the door to the yard had been left open. Sam sat on a stool by the fire, turning a couple of fowls on the spit while his mother stirred broth in a pot over the flames. Clarice had put a basket of bread, and butter and cheese on the table, and now sat with her chin in her hands, contentedly watching Edward and Francis play with the dogs in the yard.

"Look at those fools!" she exclaimed, laughing. "They are teasing poor Lion so that the animal knows not what to do."

"Call them in for supper," said her mother. "Sam, leave that and help me get the meat on the platter."

Clarice rose and went to the door.

"And tell your father, too, and Anne," added Mother. "They will be seeing to the horses."

When the fowls were on the plate and keeping warm before the fire, Sam took his place on the long bench to the left of his father at the head of the table. One day, when Edward had inherited the farm, he would sit in his father's seat. Francis climbed in beside Sam, and Edward opposite him, at his father's right hand. His father was a countryman, his brothers country boys. With them came the warm smell of cow dung and the tang of sweat-stained shirts. Edward was a stocky, muscled nineteen-year-old and Francis, at thirteen, was already as tall as Sam and almost as heavy. They did time-honoured, worthy work, and would do it all their days. But was Sam's work worthy? Even if he could not now be a farmer, should he not be doing something which offered a more predictable path through life than acting?

Sam had made a different choice from his brothers. But when he had made that choice, to join a troupe of players and live in London, his future path had seemed certain. Only a few months ago his only anxiety was that Mr Shakespeare never gave him good parts to play. But now, since he had fallen in love with Lucie, everything had changed.

"Come, Sam, eat." Smiling, Clarice passed a bowl of broth to Francis, who passed it to Sam. Then she picked up the next bowl for Mother to fill. "What are you thinking about, brother? You look as if you are a thousand miles away."

"A thousand miles away!" cried Francis. "What is a thousand miles away, Sam? The New World?"

"Nay, the New World is farther than that," his father told him good-naturedly. Then, to Clarice, "But I'll warrant that Sam is only fifty miles away, in London. The boy cannot be blamed for wishing to return there, to his acting work."

"I was not thinking of London," protested Sam, though mildly, since this was not strictly true. "I was thinking about … my family, and wondering when I will see you all again."

"Aye, the life of the theatre is chancy, right enough," replied his father. "Now, if we are all served, I will say the grace."

Sam put his hands together and bowed his head. The action was so familiar that he had done it on his first night at home as he did it now, as naturally as if he were a small boy again. But for years he had not done it. At Mistress Corrie's table, sticky with spilled ale, the three apprentices lunged for the best piece of bread the moment they entered the room, and attacked whatever piece of gristly meat or charred mackerel their landlady had provided, with the energy born of necessity. No one gave a thought to thanking the Lord for the provender. They did not even thank Mistress Corrie.

"Thank you, Lord, for our daily bread," said Father. "And may you keep our dear Samuel, and all of us, safe from harm. Amen."

Sam murmured the amen and began to eat. The food was good, and he was beloved of those who surrounded him. The feeling of being once more a child persisted. His father had shown some perception when he had said that Sam could not be blamed for thinking about going back to London – he knew it was important to his son. But *why* was it so important? Why did he so want to exchange his mother's good cooking for the unappetising messes put before him by a landlady? Or prayer for ungodliness, and a clear conscience for the ever-present dread that his furtive meetings with Lucie would be discovered?

"Do you like your broth, Sam?" asked Anne. She knelt up on the bench and leaned towards Sam, her smile showing small, gapped teeth. She was like a miniature copy of Clarice, Sam thought, in her dark gown and white cap and apron. She would, however, perhaps be prettier. "I grew the turnips for it."

"Sit down, Anne," instructed her mother. "Do you wish Sam to tell his friends in London that his sister does not know how to behave at table?"

She sat down, her eyes still on Sam's face. "You would not do that, would you, Sam?"

"Of course not." He was stabbed with guilt. He

had never mentioned Anne's name to anyone in London, save Lucie. "And the broth is very good, especially the turnips."

The fowls disappeared quickly. Clarice poured ale and everyone drank to Sam's safe journey on the morrow. In the farmhouse windows the light showed the bluish tinge of dusk. Francis rose and lit rushlights, and placed them in their holders on the walls. Sam, nibbling on a piece of cheese, was suddenly seized with the desire to be outside.

He stood up and climbed over the bench. "I am going for a walk," he announced. "I must breathe country air one last time, before I am again confined by buildings and streets."

Clarice, with a glance at her mother, stood up too. "May I go with you, Sam?" Her voice was eager though her eyes were wary. "Or do you wish to be alone?"

"You may come." Sam had no reason to forbid it. Clarice had been his confidante even when Tom had been alive. But her twin's death and Sam's departure, which came hard upon each other, had compelled her to find solace in her own company. Anne was yet too young to be companion for her. She must often, Sam realized as he watched her brushing crumbs from her apron and tidying her hair, be lonely.

"May I go, Mother, and leave this?" she asked, indicating the remains of the meal.

"Of course. The boys can help me."

"But we wish to go with Sam too!" protested Edward, swinging his legs over the bench. "Come on, Francis."

"No," said Father. "Let your brother and sister alone. They do not want the two of you snapping at their heels like curs." He waved Sam and Clarice towards the door. "Begone, then, and take a light, for it will soon be black as ink out there."

Clarice insisted upon carrying the lantern. "Let me do this small thing for my brother before he goes away again," she said as they passed through the farm gate and began to climb the hill.

"Very well," said Sam. "But when the lantern starts to feel heavy do not tell me that I am ungentlemanly."

"You are never ungentlemanly, Sam."

They walked on in silence. There was no need for discussion; both knew where they were going. There had been no opportunity in the past three days for Sam to go down to the sea, but he had resolved to do so before he departed for London, and this was his last chance. For her part, Clarice knew her brother well enough. The only remedy for the tension she detected in him this evening was the swelling and breaking of the waves.

It was not quite dark. The sky still showed a pale stripe on the horizon, changing to purplish-blue as it ascended to the heavens. The stars were not yet visible, and there was a slender moon. The lantern lit their way across the rocks, but little else. Sam handed his sister down on to the pebbled beach. The tide was almost in. Their shoes crunched as they descended to the water's edge.

Together they looked out to sea. The only sound was the lapping of the waves. Sam watched the pebbles emerge, shining, from the foam over and over again, and over and over again become submerged. It was a peaceful sight, and a peaceful sound. But his heart was not at peace.

"Clarice," he said, still looking at the horizon, "do you believe that love – true love – can overcome any obstacle?"

She thought for a while. "The love of God can, of course. But do you speak of the love between a man and a woman?"

He nodded.

"Then I cannot say. I have not felt that love."

"The one I love asked me that question once," said Sam.

Clarice turned to him. She held up the lantern, her eyes wide. "And what was your answer?"

"I said that of course I did. And I believed it when I said it. But now…"

"Have you changed your mind?"

Sam kicked at the shingle. Her words made him sound like a fool, a man who said only what his listener wished to hear. "No, I have not changed my mind. I still believe that a love such as she and I share is true. But…" He looked intently into her face. "In the future lie obstacles so high, I do not see how any love can climb them. I fear this, I confess."

"Oh, Sam." She squeezed his arm. "Come, let us walk along the shore."

She kept hold of his arm, and they set off. It was much darker. Sam took the lantern and held it before them, lighting their way along the uneven shingle beach. "My love can never marry a player," he told Clarice softly. "But she loves me because I *am* a player."

This was the first time he had said these words aloud. He had pledged his life and livelihood to the Lord Chamberlain's Men, surrendering his youth to a long apprenticeship and his manhood to hard employment, rewarded neither by a high salary nor public approval. The last four years had taught him to expect no gratitude for the hours of work the production of a play required, and to ask for no consideration, in or out of the company. Players, he had concluded long ago, were players because they *had* to be. Once the fire was in a man's blood, it would not be extinguished.

Wisely, Clarice had remained silent. Sam swallowed, took a breath and went on. "I love my life in the theatre, even more now than hitherto. Mr Shakespeare has begun to give me better parts, and I can feel my powers growing, Clarice, as surely as you see the wheat growing in the fields. I will be a good actor one day. But however good an actor I become, it will count for nothing if I cannot make my love my own. And I cannot do both."

He stopped, ashamed of the constriction in his throat. Seventeen-year-old boys did not weep in front of their fifteen-year-old sisters, even in the dark.

"Why not?" asked Clarice. "You say your lady loves you because you are a player. If you stop being a player she may not love you any more. So you must remain a player."

She made it sound very simple. But it was not. "She is not born to the life of a player's wife," he explained.

"Then she can learn," returned Clarice. "If she

herself believes that love can overcome any obstacle, she will do it willingly."

Sam tried to imagine Lucie in a cap and apron, bustling around a small parlour like Mistress Phillips, directing the servants about warming pans and chamber pots and what to buy at the market. It was impossible. "No, she will not," he told Clarice.

"Then do not marry her."

These words stung Sam. When he had first seen Lucie, she was like an angel, or a work of art. Distant, dreamlike. Then, when she had told him of her admiration for him, the painting had come alive, and he had felt as much amazement as love. He had assumed the adventure would soon be over, and he would go back to standing in William's shadow as he approached pretty girls in taverns. But when Sam had kissed Lucie, alone in his room, that meeting of both flesh and minds had convinced him that he must marry no one but her. Although there seemed no way to make this happen, Clarice's suggestion that he forget all about it was intolerable.

"I cannot live without her," he confessed.

Clarice stopped and looked up at him, the lantern flame playing upon her face. She looked agitated. "Then you must decide what is more important: your love or your livelihood. Do you not see, Sam? If she truly loves you, she will stay with you whatever happens. If she does not, then you must part."

Sam knew she was right. "I will try to behave honourably," he told her.

"When do you ever do anything else?" She smiled,

timidly at first, then wider. "And when *I* fall in love, I will bring you back here to the beach and pour out my heart as you have done. And you must not tease me."

"Of course I will not tease you," said Sam. They regarded each other for a moment. "Now, we had better turn."

As they began to walk back in the direction of the farmhouse, Clarice gazed upwards. "Oh, look, Sam! The stars are out!"

"And very beautiful they are, too." He took her arm. "Now, my dearest sister, it is vital that you do not speak of anything we have said tonight."

She nodded.

"And will you remember me in your prayers?"

"I always do. God will watch over you if you place your trust in Him and in the truth, you know."

"I hope so," said Sam. "I truly hope so."

Twelfth Night

$\mathcal{T}$he autumn, and the life of the Lord Chamberlain's Men, wore on.

The three Henrys were played regularly, with Robert Armin growing increasingly confident in the role of Falstaff. Sam watched him with admiration. Once Sir John Falstaff's padding had been strapped around his wiry body, and the beard and wig secured upon his head, Mr Armin simply *became* Sir John. Audiences were as moved by Falstaff's off-stage decease now as they would have been if Mr Kempe had played him. Mr Shakespeare, with transparent relief, raised many a glass at Mistress Turville's to the absent Mr Kempe, while congratulating Robert Armin upon his own success.

As Clarice had advised, Sam tried to place his trust in God and the truth. But God seemed to have forsaken Lucie and her aunts, still innocently imprisoned in Essex House. And how could he find the true answer to the question that prevented his sleep at night and filled his working days? Was it really a choice between

Lucie or his life as a player? If a sacrifice was to be made, was he brave enough to make it?

One November morning, when it was so cold that frost smeared the inside of the window, Sam and Robert were awakened by the noise of Nathan Field mounting the stairs three at a time. He threw open the door. "Essex House is free!"

Nathan Field was often a news-bringer, it seemed to Sam. Robert put his nose over the blanket. "What are you speaking of, you lunatic?" he demanded groggily.

"She has lifted her guard," said Nathan urgently. "Masters, this bodes well for the Lord Chamberlain's Men, does it not?"

"If 'she' is Her Majesty, you discourteous mongrel, then you had better call her by her correct title," said Robert, sitting up. He shivered violently as he spoke. "By God, this cold would freeze the fires of hell."

Sam's chest felt compressed. From the coldness of the air, but also from some other cause. "On what authority do you have this, Nathan?" he asked. "And where have you been this morning?"

"Using my wits," said Nathan, laying his finger along the side of his nose. It was a gesture they used on-stage to indicate a secret overheard. "Last night at Mistress Turville's I took no liquor, but listened to the talk of the tavern. One of the gentlemen left his tongue unguarded. He said he had heard that she – very well, Robert, *Her Majesty* – was considering lifting the guard on Essex House, and allowing the Essex family to go about freely and come to court again, even if Lord Essex himself remains imprisoned."

"Heard!" Sam forgot to hide his disappointment. *"Considering!* So in other words, you have it on *no* authority!"

Nathan regarded him curiously. "Why do you not listen to what I say before you accuse me? You asked me where I was this morning, and I have not had a chance to tell you." Wrapped in a blanket, he perched on his bed, looking like a child much younger than his fourteen years. "This morning I rose before the sun, when a freezing mist lay all around. I went and had a good look at York House, where Lord Essex is kept. More guards there than ever before. Then I dawdled up the Strand, you know, slowly like, keeping near the buildings, and quiet as a water rat. I looked at Essex House. No guards, not even one. I slipped round the back. No guards. And if it is not guarded by night, you can be sure it will not be by day."

Sam could picture Nathan making his way through the darkness in his self-appointed role of spymaster for the Lord Chamberlain's Men. He was small and quick, and even if anyone had been out at that hour, they would not have looked at a boy in an apprentice's cap, making his way to or from his employment, biting his frozen fingers and stamping his frozen toes. But Sam remained cautious. "We have only your word, Nathan," he told the younger boy.

"My word and the evidence of your own eyes," said Nathan. "Soon Lady Essex will appear in our audience again, I tell you."

Robert, who had attended to Nathan's words in silence, now turned earnestly to Sam. "I believe Nathan.

I do, Sam. Lady Essex will lose no time in advertising to the world that she is a free woman, and that her husband's conduct does not reflect upon her own."

Sam nodded. He had remembered that he must not betray before Nathan an interest in Essex House beyond that of any other member of the company. "We must take this news to Mr Shakespeare and Mr Burbage," he said, "though my guess is that they will hear it from some other source before this day is out. News, like rumour, travels fast."

"But you first heard it from me!" cried Nathan triumphantly. "I am Mercury, the messenger of the gods!" He stood up and dropped his blanket, his face full of mischief. "See my wings?" Flapping his hands behind him, he leapt about in the confined space, until, tripping over Robert's boots, he sprawled on the floor.

Sam and Robert laughed. Sam knew that his own laughter only came so readily because for the first time since the end of September, his fear for Lucie's future had diminished. It had not disappeared – that could not happen until her uncle's fate was known – but Sam's heart was lighter than it had been for many weeks. After breakfast, as he, Nathan and Robert walked briskly to the Blackfriars ferry, he watched his steamy breath and whistled, as if everything were ordinary again.

William, who lived nearer the theatre, was there before them, wearing a sheepskin jerkin and blowing on his fingers. Mr Shakespeare was there too. He had set up a writing table and stools in the curtained space at the back of the stage. Sam did not need to ask what was happening. When Nathan had cheerfully imparted the news about Essex House to Mr Shakespeare, and Mr Shakespeare had quizzed him in much the same way Sam and Robert had, Sam approached his master. "What is the new play, sir?"

"A comedy, my boy." Mr Shakespeare placed a manuscript and several sheets of blank paper on the table. "The queen commanded me to take up my quill again some weeks ago. She wishes us to present the new play at court, to celebrate the arrival of the new century."

"Is it to be performed on New Year's Eve?" asked William, scrutinizing the manuscript.

"No, on the very last night of Christmas, the fifth of January. Twelfth Night," said Mr Shakespeare. "Nathan, run for some warm ale. Sam and Robert, sit down and take up your pens. You know what to do."

The task of copying out the individual actors' parts from Mr Shakespeare's original manuscript fell to apprentices, and was supposed to be tedious. But Sam liked it, because it meant that he was the first to read the words of a new play, even if the ending of the story remained a mystery.

"Give me one of the pages, William," he said, taking his penknife from his pocket. "Writing will keep my hands warm."

Cramped and crossed through as Mr Shakespeare's handwriting was, Sam did not feel daunted by this, nor by the height of the pile of papers. He set to the work with relish, trying to make sense of the play.

It appeared that Viola, the leading lady, who would be played by William, spent most of the play pretending to be a boy. She was therefore unable to acknowledge to Duke Orsino, who would be played by Mr Phillips, that she was in love with him. Sam could easily imagine the delight William and Mr Phillips would take in acting out this situation.

Sam himself was to be Olivia, the countess with whom Duke Orsino was in love. Olivia, however, fell in love with Viola, who, of course, she assumed to be a boy. So Sam and William had some scenes of high comedy too – Olivia pursuing Viola, and Viola rejecting Olivia in order to pursue her own object of desire, Orsino. It was exactly the kind of outrageous farce the queen liked.

And the Lord Chamberlain's Men had to try especially hard to please Her Majesty at this time. Although their connection with Lord Essex had apparently so far been ignored in court circles, any play depicting English history would be very ill-advised. In commissioning a new comedy the queen had shown her intuition. Her messenger's unvoiced instruction, "Do not try anything clever, Mr Shakespeare," was obvious. And Mr Shakespeare, though clever beyond any messenger's imagination, though not perhaps the queen's, had obeyed.

As Sam wrote, he thought about Lucie. Now that the guard on Essex House had been lifted, he would soon receive a letter, and meet her again. A picture of her sprang into his mind, and hung there like the beautiful painting with which he always associated her. She was wearing an amber-coloured gown, the one she had caught her shoe in, now almost twelve months ago. Diamonds glinted in her hair and at her throat. In her eyes glowed the expression he adored – a blend of love, mockery, desire, intelligence and defiance no artist could ever truly capture.

He thought about how lovely she had looked in the Juliet cloak, and reflected that Southwark's reputation as a vice-ridden haunt of ne'er-do-wells had never been so welcome. He smiled to himself, imagining her delight when he put his plan into action. William's room was the perfect place for his next encounter with her.

A letter from Lucie eventually arrived, but it was delivered by a very different-looking Matty. Her features were pinched, her face drained of colour. "What is it?" Sam asked, dreading her answer. "Is Lady Lucie well?"

"Perfectly well," replied the maidservant. "It is I who suffer. For the past week rheumatism has kept me abed. I was able to get up today, and my mistress implored me to bring this letter. But I am in such pain, Master Sam…"

"I am very sorry to hear it," said Sam, taking her arm. "Let me walk back with you."

"That would not be wise," said Matty, trying to smile. "Though I thank you. I can manage, if I go slowly. I will wait here for your reply."

Sam went upstairs and opened the letter. Lucie was, predictably, overjoyed that Essex House had been freed, but despondent about Matty's rheumatism.

…She is not young, and I must take care of her as she takes care of me. We may not be able to correspond for a

while, but be assured I am thinking of you. My aunts tell me they do not intend to go to another play until the spring, and of course we cannot now have the players perform at Essex House, with my uncle under arrest and awaiting trial. I shall not see you in your woman's weeds for a long time. Not, perhaps, until you next play at court. I pray you are safe and well. I await your reply to this letter with impatience and love.

    Lucie

Clinging miserably to the hope that Lucie would attend the court performance on the sixth of January, Sam wrote a reply to her letter. He read her words one last time, mindful of the fact that wily Nathan Field would find anything Sam tried to hide in their room. Then, reluctantly, he destroyed the letter and all her others, one by one.

As the winter deepened so did Sam's frustration. He felt helpless. He felt as if time had slowed, or even stopped, and nothing could happen until the outcome of Lord Essex's trial was known. His relief at the lifting of the guard on Essex House had dispersed so quickly that he could not remember feeling it. He pictured the future as a sword suspended over his head, ready to dub him on his shoulder as befitted a hero, or bury itself in his heart, whichever fortune decided.

But the work of the players never ended. On a fresh, unexpectedly sunny January morning, the company gathered in the deserted Globe for a final rehearsal of the new play the queen had commissioned. They had worked very hard on it, but twenty-four hours before the performance, to everybody's bewilderment, the play still did not have a title.

Mr Shakespeare looked apologetic. "I still have not thought of anything," he confessed. Scratching his head, he read out the first line. "'If music be the food of love, play on.' You see, men, the title must be something about love. But my brain is as blank as…" He searched for a comparison. "As Sam Gilburne's face."

"Your brain is never blank, sir," said Sam loyally.

"Indeed? Do you think you can copy William Hughes's flattering ways, boy?" said Mr Shakespeare. "And stop smirking, Hughes," he added, flicking William a glance from the corners of his eyes.

Mr Heminges had a suggestion. "You or Richard could go on and say, 'We present this offering, Your Majesty, to welcome sixteen hundred, the whatever-it-is year of your illustrious reign.' You know the sort of thing, Will."

Mr Shakespeare looked at Mr Burbage. "Can we do that, Richard? Play it without calling it anything?"

"My opinion is that it needs a title." Mr Burbage made a slight bow to Mr Heminges. "Though what you will, John."

Mr Shakespeare seized upon these words. "Of course! We can call it *What You Will*!"

No one spoke. The senior members exchanged glances. They knew it was up to them to pass judgement upon this notion of Mr Shakespeare's, but all were reluctant to do so.

"What do you think?" asked Mr Shakespeare of the company at large.

"It is a meaningless title, Will," ventured Mr Phillips.

"But comedies do not need meaningful titles," replied Mr Shakespeare. "*Much Ado About Nothing* is hardly a meaningful title, is it?" He looked around the circle of doubtful faces. The eagerness slid off his face and was replaced by resignation. "All right, gentlemen, I await suggestions."

"I have one," said Thomas Pope. "We could call the play *Twelfth Night*, after the special night on which it will first be performed."

"*Twelfth Night*," repeated Mr Shakespeare, nodding. "Thank you, Tom, but I still think *What You Will* is superior."

As one man, the company protested. This solution was so obvious, each of them felt that he should have been the one to voice it.

"Why are you so stubborn, Will?" demanded Mr Burbage. "Tom's suggestion is by far the better one."

"But *Twelfth Night* is appropriate on only one day each year," said Mr Shakespeare calmly. "And we must perform the play on many other occasions."

Mr Phillips looked as if he were about to lose patience, but he controlled himself. "Supposing, for tomorrow night," he said to Mr Shakespeare, "we call it *Twelfth Night, or What You Will*, since it is not unusual practice to give a work an alternative title. And if you consider the title inappropriate for other occasions, we can simply drop the *Twelfth Night* part after tomorrow's performance."

Mr Shakespeare took his hat off, turned it round and put it back on the other way. "Very well. Let the play be called as Mr Phillips suggests. Then we can put this matter to bed, many hours, alas, before we can join it there."

He went to the front of the stage and addressed an invisible audience. "Your Majesty, Lords, Ladies, Gentles all, we present *Twelfth Night, or What You Will*." He paused, thinking. Then he turned to look at Mr Phillips. "Augustine, you have defeated me. It is too unwieldy. I shall announce the play tomorrow as *Twelfth Night*."

The senior men bowed, and Sam and the other boys followed suit. William caught Sam's eye. "Mr Phillips won the day, then," he said softly.

"He thought he had," whispered Sam in reply. "But I would wager that Mr Shakespeare preferred *Twelfth Night* all along. He is an accomplished actor, William."

The lady Olivia's dress was threaded with gold. It was a new costume, made especially for Sam. Its oversleeves draped heavily, almost reaching the floor, which was apparently the latest fashion. The petticoat was plain canvas, as the Lord Chamberlain's Men's funds did not reach to the fine undergarments of real ladies. But over it went the stiffest, most richly embroidered skirt and bodice Sam had ever worn. Gold was woven between many bright colours, depicting peacocks, ferns, even mermaids.

Sam did not understand the reason for such extravagance, but William had the answer immediately. "The Burbages are showing the queen and her courtiers that the company is earning money despite the absence of its rich friends. Yours is not the only new costume tonight, Sam."

Of course. Everything, even an actor's costume,

could hold a hidden message for courtiers who knew how to interpret it. Sam sighed as he laced the bodice over the wooden stomacher, reflecting that even without tonight's additional meaning, his golden skirt and sleeves were notable in themselves. The law clearly stated that only persons of very high birth indeed were permitted to wear cloth of gold. Everyone below who wished to adorn themselves had to be content with silk, satin, velvet and furs inferior to the sables of royalty. But the players had to create the illusion that the people on the stage were *real* kings, dukes, earls and their wives and daughters. So permission had been granted by Her Majesty for them to wear what the law decreed for the character they were playing.

Within reason, of course. Olivia's ruff was heavily starched and decorated, and scratched Sam's neck like cats' claws, but it bore no resemblance to the splendour of the ruffs worn by the real court ladies. It was certainly nothing like the spreading, jewel-encrusted collar that framed the queen's face tonight.

When Sam had lined up with the rest of the company to greet Her Majesty, he had noticed immediately how much older she appeared than last year. Her white make-up covered the true nature of her skin as successfully as his own would later cover the shadow of his beard. Her rouged lips and cheeks gave her a doll-like appearance, which, though arresting, chilled him. The power she wielded could not be farther from the vacant simplicity of a doll.

He had watched her approach the throne, turn and sit gracefully upon it, waiting while her skirts were arranged by her attendants. Then she had nodded to Mr Burbage, who, with a low bow, had led the players away to prepare for the performance.

Sam thought about the queen now as he pulled on his wig and whitened his face. This is what her ladies do for her every morning, he said to himself. This is what Lord Essex interrupted that day at Nonsuch Palace. He will never be forgiven.

Despite the small prospect of seeing Lucie in the audience tonight, his heart remained heavy. It was doubtful that she would be there, and even if she were he would have to be content with looking at her, since it was next to impossible to send her a message, or to receive one from her, without discovery. Love, strong though it was, could not repair the damage done to their chances of happiness by Lord Essex's defiance of the queen. Sam knew that this turn-of-the-century year would be the test. If Lord Essex behaved obediently, shunning his former friends, then perhaps all would be well. But if he did not, then this sixth day of January sixteen hundred might be the last Twelfth Night he ever saw.

"'If music be the food of love, play on!'" Mr Phillips's voice declaimed from the stage. Olivia did not enter for a while, so Sam had plenty of time to finish painting his lips and cheeks, and black-lining his eyes. There was no doubling in *Twelfth Night*. The company could easily run to the number of named players, and the others were acted by the musicians, hired for the performance. At rehearsals Sam had taken great pleasure in listening to Robert Armin singing the song that ended the play. It was a funny, moving little song that would probably prove very popular. Mr Armin had a better voice than Mr Kempe, he thought secretly. And he could play a lute.

Now, waiting for his entrance in his golden gown, Sam dreamed of playing a lute and singing for Lucie's delight. He watched William acting Viola acting a boy, and mused on the fact that the play was about the separation by shipwreck of a twin brother and sister. Sam thought about Clarice and Judith Shakespeare, separated from their twin brothers by more than shipwreck. William was right – the death of Judith's brother, Hamnet, still weighed heavily upon Mr Shakespeare. He had written it into his play.

Sam's entrance came. The audience laughed during Olivia's argument with the fool, played by Mr Armin. But then, when Sam had to strut petulantly to and fro across the front of the stage, he made them laugh for the wrong reasons, by stumbling over the hem of his skirt.

He had just caught sight of Lucie and Lady Rich. They sat to the left of the stage. Sam felt Lucie's eyes pierce Olivia's bodice, stomacher, corset and chemise, and strip him of his wig and make-up. She was not looking at Olivia at all, but at Sam Gilburne. She had told him he was beautiful, he remembered, as sweat formed upon his forehead and his heart moved busily in his chest. She had noticed the elegance with which he turned his head, she had said, whether he were wearing a skirt or not…

Trying to concentrate, Sam completed his strutting. The scene went on around him. Mr Armin made his exit.

Olivia's manservant, who was played by Mr Pope, entered and told Olivia that a young man (Viola in disguise) wished to see her. Sam turned. Mr Pope was obscuring his view of Lucie. He must remember his line. "'What kind o' man is he?'" came to him, though whether from the prompter or his memory he could not tell.

After this scene he was not needed for a long time. He collapsed into a chair and forced himself to think. Under his wig his scalp prickled. Perhaps Lucie *would* send him a message. Or would she wait for him to send one to her? After the performance there would be supper for the players as usual. But Lucie could not enter that gathering, and he could not enter the room where she would be entertained. He nibbled his thumbnail, wondering.

The remainder of the play seemed to Sam to last far, far longer than its two hours' duration. Sam enjoyed doing the scene where Olivia had to flirt with the disguised Viola, taking "her" for a beautiful young man, which was what William actually was, of course. The audience showed their appreciation of the cleverness of this scene by laughing loudly during it and applauding when it was over. But Sam's waits between scenes seemed endless.

After the final bow Sam changed quickly, and was wiping his make-up off when Robert, still dressed as Olivia's maid, approached him. "Did you see her, sitting with Lady Rich?" he whispered.

"Of course," confirmed Sam. "It is wonderful, is it not?"

"What is wonderful?" asked Nathan Field, picking up Sam's discarded dress and folding the precious material carefully. Sam knew he should have done this himself.

"It is wonderful that you expect to be included in a private conversation," said Robert. "Buzz, buzz, you varlet. You may fold my dress too, when I have removed it."

Nathan offered no riposte. He would never catch up with Robert and Sam in age, but the time would come when he, and they, would no longer be apprentices. When all three were working as hired men, Nathan's position in the company would be equal with theirs. His revenge, Sam predicted, would be prolonged and meticulous.

Mr Heminges appeared, tidying his cuffs. He looked very impatient. "You are not still in that skirt, are you, boy?" he asked Robert. "You are the tardiest apprentice we have ever had. Look at Sam here, changed and ready for his supper, and his costume folded." He mimed a kick at Robert's backside. "That is what you need, Goughe, and doubt me not, one day you will get it!"

Nathan Field was highly amused by this scene. While he was occupied in performing his own version of the kick at Mr Heminges's retreating back view, William passed by, still in the dress Viola wore as her true self at the end of the play. Sam saw him take something from its bodice, but did not expect what happened next. His friend embraced him, pushing something sharp-cornered between Sam's shirt and his chest. Before he released him, William whispered, close to Sam's ear, "A page gave me this for you. So you are attracting young boys now, are you?"

"Very funny." They both knew perfectly well who the piece of paper, folded very small and secured with knotted embroidery silk, was from.

Sam scrambled into his boots, smoothed his hair with impatient fingers and quitted the room before anyone could stop him. In the passageway he leaned against the wall beneath a torch and opened the note.

I will meet you in the window recess at the end of the landing above the banqueting house. It will be dark up there, so bring a lantern.

There was no greeting or signature. Lucie was either being extremely careful, or had not had time to write more. Sam did not stop to wonder if the note could be a trick. He took a lantern from its stand and mounted the stairs two at a time. As Lucie had predicted, the upstairs corridor was unlit. At the head of the stairs he held up the light and looked both ways.

She was not there. Sam stood in the darkness, hardly breathing, aware of the sound of many conversations below his feet, and a masculine voice singing to the accompaniment of bursts of laughter. He could smell roasting meat and warming wine, and the strong aroma of wood smoke from the fireplaces. As he grew used to the dark he could see the arch of the window and its many leaded panes. Beneath it he could make out a long seat, covered with tapestry cushions. Despondently he sat on it, and rested his elbows on this knees.

Lucie must be down there, amid those many voices, listening to that music. For some reason, she had not been able to escape. He wondered what to do next. He did not know what time it was, but he guessed he must have left the tiring-room at least ten minutes ago, when Mr Heminges had already been impatient to go to supper.

"Sam?"

He stood up eagerly. But the voice that had come out of the darkness was not Lucie's. It was Mr Shakespeare's.

"This is an ill-starred meeting, Sam Gilburne," he said softly.

Sam knew it. Though he must speak, his mouth was so dry he could barely form the words. "Sir, I know I am not supposed to be here, but I have good reason."

Mr Shakespeare had emerged from a room off the upstairs corridor. The light from the half open door revealed, to Sam's surprise, that his master's face was frozen with dread. "Speak, then, boy!" he demanded.

"I cannot, sir."

"You cannot speak?"

"I mean I cannot tell you why I have left the company downstairs." He wondered why Mr Shakespeare had done the same, but could not ask.

"Must I draw my own conclusion, then? That you are bent on mischief?"

"No, sir. At least you may, but I am not."

Sam could hear questioning voices from inside the room. Mr Shakespeare, keeping his eye immovably upon Sam, reassured his companions that it was merely his servant, bringing a lantern to light him downstairs. Bidding his friends farewell, he closed the door and looked into Sam's face. "You see, I am discreet, Master Gilburne. Does anyone but you and I know you are hiding here?"

"No…"

His hesitation was miniscule, but it was too late. Mr Shakespeare caught Sam's collar with both hands. His countenance was now not only fearful, but incensed. His large eyes looked larger than ever, and his perspiring brow gleamed under the light. "Speak the truth, boy! You were to meet someone, were you not? For the love of God, what possessed you to place yourself in such danger? Do you not know the situation? Have you not eyes and ears? If we players keep to our appointed place and keep our mouths shut, we will, with luck, keep our heads."

Sam was ashamed. Mr Shakespeare and Mr Burbage would take the force of the queen's wrath if she supposed for one instant that conspiracy was taking place under her own roof. "I pray you, sir, forgive my rashness," he begged. "My reason for being here has nothing to do with politics."

Mr Shakespeare's eyes glinted. Sam thought he saw relief pass momentarily across them. But then they took on the look of sharp concentration with which all the apprentices were familiar. "Then why cannot you confess it?"

"Because it involves another person, sir, who is as ignorant of this encounter as you are of that person's identity. We all three of us cannot gain by my confession. Therefore there is little point in my making it."

Mr Shakespeare let Sam's collar go. "By God, Gilburne, you should be studying Latin, not acting," he said. "You will be a lawyer yet."

At that moment the sound of footsteps – light, quick,

feminine – made both their heads turn. Lucie was approaching by way of an upper staircase. Sam saw her alight upon the landing, holding her skirts out of the way of her hastening feet. She took two steps along the landing, saw Mr Shakespeare and stopped, horror-struck.

Sam's blood buzzed in his ears. There was no time for him to do anything. In half a second Mr Shakespeare had got himself between Lucie and the staircase.

When Sam and Lucie had last met, in the servants' hallway of Essex House, Lucie had clung to him and cried like a child. Now she stood resolute, her chin tilted upwards. Her half-closed eyes regarded Mr Shakespeare as she might any gentleman who came into her presence unannounced. Sam realized with a rush of pride that if *he* did not betray their association, neither would she.

"Who affronts me in this way, barring my path?" Lucie dropped the heavy material of her skirt, which hit the wooden floor with a soft thump, like the sound of the closing curtains at the back of the stage at the Globe. "Speak, man, and explain yourself."

Mr Shakespeare took the lantern and held it near his face. "It is I, William Shakespeare, my lady."

When Mr Shakespeare was at the lowest point of his low bow, Lucie's eyes met Sam's over his bent back. Their expression said "I love you" so clearly that Sam stepped hurriedly back into the shadows. He could not keep his countenance as innocent as the situation demanded.

Lucie extended her hand. "Pray arise, sir, and let me look upon the face of a man truly gifted by God. I am very pleased to meet you again."

Mr Shakespeare, knowing that Sam could no more escape down the stairs than Lucie could escape up them, made no haste. He straightened up, and, kissing Lucie's hand, thanked her for her compliments.

"What brings you up here, Mr Shakespeare, when you might be at supper with the rest of your company below?" she asked. "And this apprentice here," she added, indicating Sam with a contemptuous nod. "What is his business here? I hope I shall not be obliged to report unregulated meetings."

"I had legitimate dealings with the gentlemen who sit in that room there," said Mr Shakespeare, indicating the door. "The Lord Chamberlain, on Her Majesty's orders, wished to congratulate me on the play. So he took the opportunity to finish some paperwork we have had outstanding these three months. And my boy came with me, to assist me. We are on our way down to supper now, are we not, Sam?"

"Ah." Lucie fleetingly looked ready to laugh. Everything Sam had told her about Mr Shakespeare was unfolding itself before her. Stupidly, Sam felt proud of him, as if Sam were the master and Mr Shakespeare the apprentice. It was clear they all knew the truth, but like the play-maker he was, Mr Shakespeare spun an effortless web of pretence. "I had better go down to my own supper," said Lucie, "before my aunt comes to look for me."

Mr Shakespeare bowed again. "I bid you good night, my lady, and so does Master Gilburne."

"Farewell, my lady," said Sam, bowing.

Lucie began to go downstairs. Sam watched the

embroidered silk of her gown crumple, and then straighten, then crumple again behind her as she trod on each stair. When she reached the bottom of the first flight, she turned. Sam could just see her in the lantern light. "Farewell, gentlemen," she said. "And God keep you."

"Come, Sam," said Mr Shakespeare. "Let us go down."

With a last look at Lucie's glowing face, Sam followed him.

"As for the lady you were supposed to meet tonight, Sam…" Mr Shakespeare remarked as they descended. They were still within earshot of Lucie, who had begun on the second flight. "Since she has evidently abandoned your tryst, so must you. It is the only way for a gentleman's pride to remain unpricked."

Sam blushed. "Yes, sir. Thank you, sir."

When they reached the bottom of the stairs Mr Shakespeare spoke again. "Now, be off with you to supper. And if you should see your lady-love passing by, be sure to doff your cap and bow. You are an apprentice yet, and will be until your other masters and I say otherwise. Do not, for your own sake, forget that."

Exit Lucie

On the opposite bank the two theatres flew their flags. At the Rose, the Admiral's Men would later that day present *Doctor Faustus*. But despite the popularity of Christopher Marlowe's tragic, magic play, Sam knew that the larger crowd would be at the Globe. Playbills had been advertising all week that in honour of the first anniversary of that playhouse's grand opening, *Julius Caesar* was to be revived.

This play had not been seen since the previous autumn, and during that time its fame had spread. People had told their friends of its spectacle. Its thrilling speeches had been inaccurately repeated in taverns all over London. Mr Shakespeare may be a good playwright, Sam concluded as he watched the flags, but he and the Burbage brothers were good managers too. Their eight-month "neglect" of such a well-received play had been wise.

The Lord Chamberlain's Men were having another busy summer. Over the past few weeks Sam had found himself performing so many parts in so many plays, he had ceased asking which was next. He knew all his different characters' lines so well that he could put on whichever costume the wardrobe master thrust into his hands and make his entrance with confidence. His eighteenth birthday had passed. Although his seniors had not yet seen fit to promote him, he considered himself an apprentice only in name.

Sam and William were sitting in the sunlight on the steps to the Blackfriars ferry. It was Saturday morning.

"I am sure Lord Essex will come to *Julius Caesar* this afternoon," declared William. "It is more than a week now since his trial. Imagine, Sam, how high his spirits must be! And when he is high-spirited, he always finds a way to make a public spectacle of himself."

Sam wondered how *he* would feel if he had spent nine months under threat of the queen's terrible vengeance, then been tried and, miraculously, freed. Lord Essex must daily be on his knees, thanking God for this deliverance. Surely he would curb his "high-spirited" behaviour after such a narrow escape?

"He will not come," said Sam. "I have said it before and I will say it…"

"No, please, Sam, not again!" pleaded William.

"Again," continued Sam. "Neither he nor anyone in his circle will ever set foot in the Globe."

William took off his hat, which was a new one, with a plume like the hat Lord Southampton had given Mr Shakespeare. In the year since William had ceased to be obliged to wear an apprentice's cap, his collection of hats had become almost as large as that of the Earl of

Southampton himself. He held the hat at arm's length, admiring it.

"Then I will say again what I have said a thousand times too," he told Sam. "Imprisonment and trial have not changed his nature. Now that he is free, he wishes to appear in public. Everyone he considers important will be gathered at the play, and since he is unable to associate with them at the Palace of Whitehall, he will do so at the Globe. If I know Lord Essex, he is planning to out-Caesar Caesar. He will appear more splendidly attired than any emperor, and with more sycophants in his wake. You mark my words."

Sam did not dare to mark William's words, though he wished them true. "Do you think he will he bring his ladies?" he asked cautiously.

"Lady Essex and Lady Rich would not miss it for the world."

"But Lucie? Why should they bring her?"

"Because she will not allow them to leave her behind." William gave Sam one of his brightest smiles, and put his hat back on. "*I* would not like to be on the receiving end of that young lady's persuasive arts, and her loving aunts must be more helpless even than I. You mark—"

"I know, your words," said Sam.

He knew William's confident prediction was kindly meant, but he could not help feeling despondent. After the elaborate farce she had played out with Sam and Mr Shakespeare on Twelfth Night, Lucie had vanished. No letters had arrived, by Matty or anyone else, and no one from Essex House had attended the playhouse.

Last week, news of the favourable outcome of Lord Essex's trial had become known. With trembling legs and drumming heart Sam had scanned each day's audience, picturing the quick turn of Lucie's head when she saw him. But the Essex party had not come, and still Lucie did not write.

Sam could no longer keep his fears from William. He put his chin in his hands and looked across the river. To his shame, tears pricked his eyes. "She will not come, William," he said. "I have neither seen nor heard from her since Twelfth Night."

After a careful pause, William said, "Do you suspect a waning of her affections?"

"No, no!" replied Sam hastily. "But I *do* suspect she is being kept out of society. Or perhaps she has been sent back to the north-country, for her safety."

"That is understandable."

Sam nodded dejectedly. "I shall never see her again." He could not look at William, but he took the grubby handkerchief his friend offered. Humiliated but grateful, he blew his nose. "Do not exert yourself to help me further, William," he said with what he hoped was finality, "though I am grateful for what you and Robert have done in the past. I must bear her loss as best I can."

William tried to speak, but Sam suppressed him. "No, do not protest. It is now a year and a half since I first set eyes on her, and almost six months since I last did so. I have the memory of that year, William, to cherish for ever."

The ferry was ready to leave. William followed Sam down the steps, and, as they boarded the boat, Sam saw the resignation on his friend's face. William would never mention Lucie's name again unless Sam did so first. The adventure was over.

A combination of misery and recklessness rushed over him. "Come, Mark Antony, what say you to a wager?" he suggested. "I will lay a shilling against Lucie being in the crowd this afternoon. If she appears, you will be the richer by a shilling, and I the happier by a … a…"

A vision of the triumphant return of Lord Essex and Lord Southampton from their military victory in Cádiz, four years ago, came into his mind. It had taken place when he had been in London only a few weeks, and was the most spectacular sight he had ever seen. "A chest of Spanish treasure," he concluded, "and ten Barbary horses."

Sam had to be content with the shilling he won off William. The Earl of Essex, as his friend had predicted, *did* attend the anniversary performance of *Julius Caesar*. But he was not accompanied by any women. Lord Southampton sat by his side, looking no more chastened by recent events than Lord Essex. Sam tried to soften the word that leaped into his mind when he saw Lucie's uncle, but could not. He looked arrogant. If anything, more arrogant than ever before. He seemed assured that the queen would soon lift his banishment, and that he could win back the affections of the London crowd as easily as Mark Antony would win over the Roman citizens in today's play. Ringleted, perfumed and elaborately dressed, he beamed as the audience cheered.

"He looks very satisfied with himself," observed Robert in a whisper. It was the point in the play where Caesar was about to be murdered, and the Roman wives did not appear again. Robert and Sam were in the tiring-room, helping each other remove their feminine robes and put on their citizens' togas. "And Lord Southampton cannot keep his eyes off William. Did you notice?"

Sam had not, but could believe it. "Perhaps his lordship will make William a gift of that outrageous hat he is wearing," he whispered to Robert. "That would be the pinnacle of William's existence, though such a gift might not come *quite* free of charge."

Robert, stifling laughter, looked at him approvingly. "It is pleasing to see you merry again, Sam."

"Have you seen Lord Essex?" came William's excited whisper. His character, Mark Antony, was off-stage while Caesar was being killed. He gathered Robert and Sam around the spyhole. "And look at the gentlemen he has with him!"

Sam looked up to where Lord Essex sat in the gallery. He saw Lord Southampton on one side of him and Lord Mountjoy, the lover of Lady Rich, on the other. Behind Lord Southampton sat Sir John Harrington, who had often attended court performances and spoken to the boys afterwards. Beyond that, he realized with a quickening heart, he recognized no one in Lord Essex's party. "Who are they?" he asked William.

William's face held an expression Sam recognized. It meant "something exciting is happening and I am thrilled to be part of it". This, coupled with the Roman robes he wore, and the circlet around his golden hair, made him resemble an over-eager girl dressed for her first ball. "I do not know all of them," he admitted, "though I can name the Earl of Sussex and the Earl of Bedford, and I think that is the Earl of Rutland sitting beside Lord Mountjoy. Sir Christopher Blount is there too – the one in the black hat – and Sir Charles Danvers and his brother. Some of these gentlemen accompanied Lord Essex to Ireland, but even those who did not have incurred Her Majesty's displeasure."

"What have they done?" asked Robert.

"They are on Lord Essex's side in his feud with Sir Robert Cecil," explained William. "And Lord Essex bestowed knighthoods on some of them without permission. But the point is, every man Lord Essex has brought here today is, like himself, *under banishment from the queen's presence.*"

Sam and Robert looked at each other. "And they are watching a play about the killing of a ruler," whispered Sam, unthinking.

"Shh!" warned William and Robert in unison.

At that moment a roar arose from the audience – the roar that marked the murder of Caesar. William put his eye again to the spyhole. "They are all standing. They are all cheering. Oh … I must go on!"

Hitching up his robes, he hurried back to the stage. A few minutes would pass before Sam and Robert were required to be citizens. Sam stood in a daze, trying to gather his wits. He remembered how he had waited behind another stage on Twelfth Night, thinking about how sixteen hundred would be a test year for Lord Essex. Now, several months later, it was becoming clear that his lordship had no intention of passing any test of humility, loyalty or even common sense. Did the man not understand how dangerous his actions were, and not only for himself?

The body of Caesar, which was really Mr Burbage, was carried off the stage by William and Nathan. "Come on," urged Robert, pulling Sam on to the stage.

The play went on. The citizens of London in the pit howled louder than the citizens of Rome on the stage as their loyalties were swayed this way and that by Mark Antony's persuasive words. Sam watched William strutting and mincing, bellowing and cooing, in absolute command of the scene. The gossiping William who had rushed into the tiring-room had vanished. In his place stood a mature actor who would one day rival Mr Richard Burbage himself. During his first year as a hired man, Sam reflected, William had certainly proved a sound return on the Burbage brothers' investment.

After the performance there was revelry, fuelled as always by satisfaction at another successful presentation and anticipation of the next one. But today's celebration was tinged with something more. Mr Burbage and the other sharers in the Lord Chamberlain's Men, with effusions of relief, welcomed the return of their esteemed patrons.

Lord Southampton responded in his characteristic way, flinging one arm around Mr Shakespeare's shoulders and the other around William's waist, and kissing them both. Mr Shakespeare angled his face so that his lordship's lips landed on his cheek, but not so William. Sam watched unconcerned; he was more tolerant of such displays of affection than when he was younger and had not yet met Lucie. But the sight made him even more despairing, if that were possible, of ever kissing her again.

"Madness! Utter madness!" Sam heard Lord Southampton say. He was surrounded by four or five of the gentlemen William had named, as well as Mr Phillips and Mr Pope. "Tell me, gentlemen," the earl continued, "why would anyone in sound mind advise the queen of England to free a scoundrel like Essex?"

There was laughter, then Sir Charles Danvers spoke. "We all know the queen's preference for Lord Essex. She has forgiven his misdeeds before."

"Is it true that she once boxed his ears?" someone asked.

"Certainly," cut in the Earl of Rutland. "So violently that he could not hear properly all day. He often repeats the story, and of course the blows get harder with each repetition."

The gathering laughed again. "Anyway," went on Sir Charles, "the queen will never make up her mind about Essex – he is too near her heart. Consider: Sir Robert Cecil, who would have Essex condemned to death tomorrow if he could, says, 'Lord Essex must be charged with treason!' The queen says, 'No, misgovernance is sufficient.' Cecil says, 'Throw him into the Tower!' But the queen says, 'No, public humiliation is sufficient.' And the best way to achieve that, gentlemen, is to banish him

– and us – from all her palaces. The entire affair smacks of feminine fickleness."

"Your vulgar notions about Her Majesty and Lord Essex will cost you dear one day, Charles," observed another of the gentlemen in the party, whose name Sam did not know. He was young, good-looking and fashionably dressed, as they all were.

"I am a friend to Lord Essex, and I defy you to say otherwise," said Sir Charles. He had stopped smiling. "A jest is merely a jest among friends."

"The queen is beloved of us all," said the young man. "But her power is great. Beware such jests, I beg you."

Sir Charles bowed stiffly. He did not speak.

"We are all friends to Lord Essex, and to Her Majesty," said Lord Southampton, adjusting his lace cuffs. "But whoever decided upon our banishment, if they think we are to be called to heel like dogs, they are mistaken. Lord Essex has been misjudged. It is all the work of that villain Cecil."

Sam felt guilty, like an eavesdropper who had heard the opposite of what he would have desired. The conversation had gone beyond banter between friends. It was a hard thought, but he forced himself to think it. The Lord Chamberlain's Men needed the patronage of these men, untrustworthy though they were. But this meant that the company stood on the brink of falling into even worse disrepute than all companies of actors endured.

Lucie, too, was caught in a place from which there was no escape. Lady Rich, in whose care she had been placed, was banished from court. Her family, whom she loved, bore the disgrace of a man who seemed bent on arousing suspicion and distrust. Sam, whom she also loved, was part of the profession that appeared to condone Lord Essex's actions. Wherever she turned, no one could offer her refuge.

"Gilburne! Where is Sam Gilburne?"

The voice belonged to Mr Phillips. His beaming face, the eyes still outlined with black paint from his recent portrayal of Brutus, appeared. He slapped Sam's shoulder. "Sam, I bring you most excellent tidings."

Robert nudged Sam with a sharp elbow. Even the curiosity of Lord Southampton, who scarcely ever even looked at Sam, was caught. Amused, the earl stilled the chatter of his friends.

"Your days as an apprentice are over, Sam," announced Mr Phillips. "I am charged by Mr Burbage to tell you that from today you are a hired man of the Lord Chamberlain's Men. And, if I may say so without reddening your face, as skilful an addition to the company as any of us could wish. Come, let us shake hands upon it."

Sam gripped Mr Phillips's hand, embarrassment eclipsed by regard for this man who had ever been his friend. Sam's first lodging had been in the Phillips household, where Mistress Phillips had understood his homesickness and made sweetmeats for him with her own hands. And Sam's first appearance on the stage had been under the guidance of Mr Phillips, who had also punished his misdemeanours, small though they were. As they shook hands now upon the ending of that relationship, Sam saw that in this gifted, highly intelligent man he would always have a supporter.

"I thank you, sir," was all Sam managed to blurt out before he found himself being applauded by a circle of aristocratic and knighted gentlemen. He bowed to them, feeling foolish. This moment, after many years of anticipation, had come so unexpectedly that Sam did not know how to conduct himself. And his confusion was increased by the memory of Clarice's unforgettable words: "You must decide what is more important, your love or your livelihood."

"Hear this!" Every head turned to see Mr Cuthbert Burbage using a sword to strike repeatedly one of the pillars that held up the canopy over the stage. "Men of the company, hear this!"

Mr Shakespeare, whom Sam had not seen since Lord Southampton's congratulatory kiss had landed upon his cheek, appeared upon the stage. His feet dragged. He looked very weary. Upon his face was the same expression as Mr Burbage wore. Sam could see that these two senior sharers had received a blow every bit as severe as those Mr Burbage was inflicting upon the pillar.

"For God's love, Will, what is the matter?" asked Mr Phillips.

Mr Shakespeare hung his head. "Cuthbert will tell you," he said. "You may stop that now, Cuthbert. Everyone is listening."

"We have just now received a communication from the Master of the Revels," announced Mr Burbage importantly. "He has decided that with immediate effect the presentation of plays is to be restricted to two performances a week."

There was a puzzled pause. "Two performances in each theatre, I take it?" asked Mr Heminges.

Mr Shakespeare and Mr Burbage shook their heads. "No, John, two performances in total," explained Mr Burbage. "We must negotiate with the Admiral's Men, and every other company at present vying for the attention of the theatre-going public, before we can play anything, on any day."

Slowly, the news sank in. It was early June, the beginning of summer. Last year, eleven or twelve performances had taken place each week at the Globe during July, August and September. This year the company would be lucky to be able to do one performance in two weeks. And Sam had this minute been made a hired man, whose wages would add to their expenses.

"Mr Shakespeare, sir, I will have my hired man status held off until after this restriction is lifted," he said before his nerve could fail him.

"You will do no such thing," replied Mr Shakespeare. "You have earned your hire and salary, and will receive it." He turned to the company. "The reason for the Master of the Revels's decision is unclear. Although I can speculate as well as the next man what it might be, I do not choose to make my opinions public, and would advise you all to do the same. At least the playhouses are not closed down completely, as they are in plague years."

This comparison was carefully chosen. Sam could see that Mr Shakespeare's polite countenance concealed a spirit oppressed by events. When plague brought death to the city, the theatres were closed to lessen the spread of infection. But now infection of a different kind was alarming the authorities. The Master of the Revels clearly suspected that theatres were breeding grounds for anti-government conspiracy. Within a week of the trial, the opportunities for Lord Essex and his followers to parade before large crowds had been severely restricted. His popularity was his greatest asset; it must not be given a platform.

"Mr Cuthbert and Mr Richard Burbage, Mr Armin, Mr Phillips, Mr Heminges, Mr Pope," continued Mr Shakespeare. "Will you accompany me to consult with the Admiral's Men? They have this afternoon given *Doctor Faustus*. They will be as anxious as we are to know when they can next present that play. We must speak urgently. As for the rest of you, let us meet as usual on Monday morning, here at the Globe. All may yet be well."

The gathering began to disperse. Sam watched Lord Essex twitch his cloak over one shoulder and lay his hand upon the hilt of his sword prior to appearing outside the building. His face, framed by its fashionable curled locks and plumed hat, was as inscrutable as Sam had ever seen it. But he must be aware – how could any man in his wits not be? – that it was his own reckless behaviour that had brought calamity upon those who had always considered him a friend.

Sam bowed along with everyone else as Lord Southampton and the other gentlemen took their leave. Lord Essex, who had lingered to exchange a few last words with Mr Shakespeare, passed by alone. Sam bowed; the earl did not look at him.

The task of clearing up after the play awaited, but Sam had not progressed far towards the tiring-room when he found his hand grasped by Mr Shakespeare. "Master Gilburne, welcome to the company as a hired man," he said warmly.

"Thank you, sir," said Sam.

Mr Shakespeare released Sam's hand and took hold of Robert's. "And good work this afternoon, Robert."

Mystified, Robert gazed after Mr Shakespeare. "But I hardly do anything in *Julius Caesar*," he said to Sam. "Do you think he is losing his wits?"

"Maybe," said Sam, keeping his fingers tightly closed around the folded paper Mr Shakespeare had left in his hand. "But maybe not."

The Player

Essex House, 12 June 1600

Dearest, dearest Sam,

I beg you, do not think that my long silence means I have ceased to love you. But Sam, we are discovered. I have failed in my duty to you. On the night I last saw you, I told Lady Rich that I love you. I have no right to demand your forgiveness, but I hope you love me enough to give it.

Under the stage, where he and Robert had offered to store some Roman props that would not be needed again for a while, Sam sat cross-legged on the floor. He did not feel anger when he read Lucie's words, nor righteous indignation. He did not even fear that he would be punished. He felt only relief that Lucie still loved him enough to engineer a way to send him a letter. It showed that although she could have fled back to Northumberland, she had not done so. Her courage, he was obliged to conclude, was no less profound than her affection.

When you and Mr Shakespeare left me that night I listened to what he said to you on the stairs. I know he meant me to hear him, and I thank him. Because of his words, I knew he would help us. If you are reading this, my dearest, he already has.

I went back to the hall where the queen was entertaining her guests. But suddenly I found myself in tears. I was overwrought, perhaps, from the strain of everything that has happened. And seeing you had reminded me how beautiful you are, and how much I love you. All my fears arose about whether we will ever be together without deception. I could not control the tears. Some ladies came to see what was the matter. I had to pretend I was unwell. Of course, they summoned Lady Rich, who took me home immediately, and Matty put me to bed.

Lady Essex was content with my explanation of a bad headache, but Lady Rich was not. Sitting by my bedside, she said that she could tell the difference between tears of sickness and tears of love. "Who is your love?" she asked me. "Is he fair? Is he dark? Can you tell his voice in a thousand others, and feel the touch of his hands long after he has left you?"

Oh, Sam, I could not help it. It was such a relief, and such a joy to speak of you. My aunt was so sympathetic, so kind and agreeable, I forgot to be on my guard. When she asked your name, I gave it. But when she understood that you were a player in the Lord Chamberlain's Men, she began to scold me so fiercely that I had to bite on the bedcovers to stop myself crying out and waking the children.

She has forbidden our correspondence, and threatened poor Matty with God's vengeance. She is clever, Sam. She has calculated that it must have been you I was meeting that day at the Curtain, when I pretended to be helping a young girl in trouble. Luckily, I did not tell her that since then I have been to your room.

She has told Lady Essex about you, and has said things to me which are too distressing to repeat. She threatened to tell my parents, and Lord Essex too. You can imagine my feelings, Sam, as I waited for the consequences of this for Mr Shakespeare's company. Day after day, I wept to think of the number of innocent and loyal young men I had brought trouble upon.

But I found an unexpected ally in my Lady Essex. She said that she saw no profit in causing her husband, or my parents, further anxiety. "Lucie's enforced separation from this player is severe enough punishment," she told Lady Rich. "Let us do no more, but introduce her to as many young gentlemen of suitable status as we can. Their attentions will soon make her forget her folly."

How little she knows me! But I am grateful to her for her leniency. Of course, the Globe is the last place either of my aunts will allow me to go, so when Lord Essex announced his intention to attend the play this afternoon, I seized my chance.

I will ask my uncle to deliver this letter discreetly to Mr Shakespeare. When he asks me why I am writing to such a man, I will pretend that I am expressing my admiration for his poetry, or some such. I will beg him not to tell my aunts that I am unpacking my girlish heart to Mr Shakespeare, as it would embarrass me. Lord Essex is always ready for a little subterfuge, as you may imagine. And I am sure that Mr Shakespeare's quick wits will ensure that the letter finds its way to you.

Now there is no time to write more. My uncle's horse is already saddled. I love you, Sam, I love you so much. Do not let me wait in vain for an answer.

Lucie

Do not let me wait in vain for an answer. Sam read the words again. Then he read them once more before folding up the letter and putting it inside his shirt.

But how was he to get a letter to her? Lucie might have persuaded her uncle to be an unwitting go-between, but for a mere player to take such liberties was insupportable. Equally unseemly was the notion that Mr Shakespeare, Sam's master, should be his messenger. What excuse did Mr Shakespeare have to go to Essex House? None that would not cause Lucie's aunts to be suspicious. The letter would never reach her. Lady Rich might even have Mr Shakespeare chased away before he got within a yard of the door. At any other time this thought would have made Sam smile. But now it made the back of his neck sweaty.

Robert came in with an armful of Roman scrolls. Sam watched him fetch an empty box from the depths of the dark space under the stage. He watched him fetch another one. He considered for a minute, and then he spoke.

"Robert, hear me. Lady Rich has found out about Lucie and me. Lucie is unable to write to me directly, so she gave this letter to her uncle to pass to Mr Shakespeare, and Mr Shakespeare passed it to me."

Robert's astonishment turned into a grin. "Ha! What a proper champion of love Mr Shakespeare is!" He began to arrange scrolls in one of the boxes. "I never would have thought it!"

"Robert, have you ever read any of his plays?"

"Ha!" was Robert's considered reply.

"Mr Shakespeare has known about Lucie for some time," Sam went on, "though he has never mentioned her to me since the night he made the discovery. He must think me the most rash, muddy-mettled rascal that ever lived."

"No he does not," encouraged Robert. "Mr Shakespeare might not say anything, but he understands everything. Are you going to write back to her?"

"If you will tell me how to deliver the letter, my fine friend."

Robert closed the lid of the box. In a sudden rush of appreciation of Robert in all his simplicity, Sam clasped Robert's arm. "I will do anything to win her, Robert," he told him urgently, realizing the incontrovertible truth of this as he said it. "Anything at all. I have had many months of doubt, when I wondered whether she and I would ever find a way to be together, but now I am resolved. My voice has been silenced and my hand stayed by Lady Rich's disapproval, but I will bear whatever punishment she devises for me if it means I can see Lucie even *once* more."

Robert's childlike eyes were troubled. But as they looked closely at Sam's face a very unchildlike expression came into them. He sat down on a "Roman" footstool. "Of what, exactly, does Lady Rich disapprove?" he asked in his careful way. "That Lucie has a lover, or that you are of low rank?"

"My low rank," admitted Sam, sitting on a box. "Lady Rich is no fool. Although she may be out of favour with the queen, she is known throughout England as an intelligent, wise and worthy woman."

"And a liberal-minded one, too," observed Robert, suddenly alert.

Sam nodded. He had no experience of Robert getting to an idea before himself or William, but circumstances required that all contributions be heard. "She is the mistress of Lord Mountjoy though she is married to Lord Rich, and makes no attempt to pretend otherwise. What of it?"

"Well, in exercising her guardianship over her niece, would she not encourage Lucie to search for true love such as she herself has found with Lord Mountjoy? Surely, a young, gentlemanly suitor *whom Lucie likes* will be welcome at Essex House?"

Sam's heart began to race. Suddenly, he knew what was in Robert's mind. "Indeed," he breathed, as much to himself as to Robert. "Indeed he would."

"It is as clear as day what we should do," declared Robert. "And if William were here *he* would tell me how clever I am, even if you do not."

"You *are* clever," Sam told him. "That I will never deny."

"Ha! Now, listen. Has Lady Rich ever spoken at length to you?"

"No," confirmed Sam, his excitement growing. "Nor you, I will wager. She barely looks at us, except when we are on stage, and then we look like girls."

"Quite so!" said Robert, with something as near to triumph in his voice as his modest nature would allow. "Like everyone else these days, she only looks at William."

"William has traded anonymity for glory," said Sam,

thinking fast. "But anonymity is sometimes the more valuable possession, is it not?"

"Quite so!" said Robert again, laughing.

"But what about Lucie?" This thought suddenly occurred to Sam. "Would she wish us to risk bringing further punishment upon her?"

Robert had stopped laughing but was still smiling. "If she dotes on you as much as she declares, do you not think she will comply with any scheme of ours, however reckless?"

Sam considered. "Recklessness is not in her nature," he decided, "but courage is. And she always has her wits about her. If we *were* to do this, she would be a ready accomplice."

"Then let us do it!" cried Robert. "It will be an adventure!"

"Your taste for adventure has already scarred your face, my friend," warned Sam.

"I care not two straws for that," said Robert stoutly. He rose, pulling Sam with him. "Come, let us to William, and tell him. He will be so astounded his eyes will pop out of his head."

"No they will not," Sam told him as they departed. "He will say, 'So you have decided to use your acting skills for something worthwhile after all, Master Gilburne, have you? Though of course *I* could do it far better.'"

Sam and Robert waited impatiently for the darkness to arrive.

"We should be doing this in September, or even October," grumbled Robert, who had been watching the sky from the window of their room for the last hour.

"Perhaps *you* can wait three months to see Lucie, but I cannot."

It was two days later. Sam was as nervous as he had ever been before any stage entrance. Perhaps more, since this was no play. Unable to rely upon Mr Shakespeare's pen, he had to devise his own part.

"If we do not go soon it will be so late that everyone in the house will be abed," said Robert. "And although Nathan usually stays out until after midnight, tonight he may come back early, and that would spoil everything."

"Very well. I am ready." Sam joined Robert at the window. "Do you think she is watching this sky from her own window?"

"What if she is?" asked Robert.

"You speak as a man who has never been in love."

"I hope that when I *do* fall in love," returned Robert moodily, "I will not subject my friends to such non-sensical observations. The sky is the sky, whether she is looking at it or not. And that is an end on it."

Sam was glad to laugh. It was hard to be amused and fearful at the same time. "You are better than strong liquor for making a man feel better," he told Robert. "Come, you go first."

He followed Robert downstairs. It was after ten o'clock, and the day's work was over for ordinary folk. Some, like Nathan Field, who never seemed to sleep, were in the tavern. But at this hour it was mostly gentlemen, who had sufficient leisure to keep late hours, who walked abroad. Dressed as they were, the boys attracted scant attention from the few passers-by.

To his surprise, Sam did not feel self-conscious. When he and Robert had raided the costume baskets last night and, after an orgy of trying-on, had selected the garments they considered would best create the illusion, he had felt as he always did when he put on a costume. He was an actor, hiding his real self behind clothes, masks and make-up. But now, striding along with a plumed hat on his head, a velvet cloak lined with taffeta hanging from his shoulders and a sword in a gilded scabbard by his side, Sam did not feel like an actor. He felt as if he had been born to wear such clothes.

As they neared the Strand the streets remained almost deserted. A carriage passed by. Bravely Robert tipped his hat to the occupants, who tipped theirs in acknowledgement. Emboldened by this success, when they passed a pair of well-dressed youths of about their own age, one on horseback, one walking beside, Sam nodded to the mounted one. Amazingly, the youth touched his hat and nodded back, and his companion did the same.

"This is easy," said Robert in a low voice.

"Indeed it is," replied Sam. "As the old saying goes, clothes maketh the man. Pray Matty does not answer the door, though, and immediately give us away."

"I need no reminder to pray, Sam!"

Essex House stood silhouetted against the blue-black sky. On the street side, the only lights were in upstairs windows. Sam guessed the windows of the main ground floor rooms faced the river.

Robert inspected the coat of arms above the door.

His right hand went to his sword. "Is this definitely the house?"

"Yes," said Sam. The same tension that Robert evidently felt had risen in his own throat. "I have been here before, though I did not come to this door."

There was still time to run away. But Sam's desire to show Lucie the strength of his love drove away the temptation. He knocked loudly upon the door with a gloved fist. Nothing happened.

"Knock again, louder," instructed Robert. "Do it with the hilt of your sword."

"Robert, this is the dwelling place of a man recently tried for crimes against Her Majesty's government," said Sam patiently. "In the circumstances, do you honestly think it would be prudent for me to draw my sword, even to knock on a door?"

The prospect of being challenged silenced Robert. Sam took off his glove and knocked again.

The cover of a small square door within the larger one slid open, wide enough for a manservant to show his face. In the Essex household, evidently, strangers were quizzed before they entered. As they had rehearsed, Robert took charge.

"Good evening, master," he said to the man. To Sam's relief, he spoke confidently, and remembered not to touch his hat. "Is this the residence of Lord Essex?"

The man's face remained inscrutable. "Who wishes to know?"

"My name is Cyril Mountbray, and this is Sir Henry Daines, of Northumberland."

Still unmoved, the man looked at Sam. Sam gave

an almost imperceptible nod, as he had seen Lord Southampton do when unable to avoid acknowledging an underling.

"I am this gentleman's cousin," went on Robert. "We have travelled a great distance in order to pay this visit to an acquaintance of ours, Lady Lucie Cheetham, daughter of Lord Cheetham, also of Northumberland. Is she at home?"

The man still did not unlock the door. A conscientious servant, he would not allow these two young gentlemen in without sanction from his superiors. "It is late to call, sir," he said to Robert. "And if you have travelled so far, might I not summon the ostler to feed and water your horses?"

"No need," said Robert. "Our horses are stabled at the inn where we have put up for the night." His invention exhausted, he turned to Sam. "Are they not, Sir Henry?"

"Indeed they are." Sam took a step nearer the manservant, who did not flinch. "Hear me, master," he said to him in an authoritative tone. "My cousin and I must leave for Dover tomorrow, from where we are to sail for France. When Lord Cheetham heard that we would be passing through London, he gave us a message for his daughter. He would not brook the intervention of a third party – he is aware that these are troubled times for his wife's relatives – so we beg leave to deliver his letter personally. We must not incur his lordship's displeasure."

Sam's guesswork proved correct. A lord ranked more highly than a knight, as the man well knew. Lucie had never told Sam the name of her father, but if he had not been at least a lord, her own name would not have been preceded by "Lady". The servant could not obstruct the wishes of a higher-ranking person than the one who stood before him.

"Lord and Lady Essex have retired for the night," he said, "but I believe Lady Rich and Lady Lucie Cheetham are within. Pray enter, and I will see if they will receive you at this late hour."

He closed the small sliding door and opened the main one, bowing as Sam and Robert passed, then bolted the door. They were shown into a large apartment on the river side of the house. Despite the warm night, its windows were tightly secured. That the Essex household took no risks was becoming increasingly clear. Sam began to feel very hot.

The servant departed, closing the door. Robert tried to speak, but Sam suppressed him. Soft, but unmistakably masculine footsteps approached the other side of the door and stopped outside it. The muffled clink of a sword was heard as the guard took up his position.

"How warm it is in here!" said Sam. "We might trouble her ladyship for a quart of ale, do you not think? I am fatigued almost to collapsing with today's ride, and we have another tomorrow, though the road to Dover is a good one, of course."

"Let us hope the innkeeper provides a good breakfast," replied Robert. Beneath the wide brim of his hat, he was grinning and winking. Sam stepped between him and the keyhole.

"Gentlemen!"

The door was flung open, and Lady Rich appeared. She looked thinner, and her hair, though still golden, had not the lustre of the day she had sat in the carriage and waved to the crowd at Tilbury Dock. The strain of recent events was telling on everyone. To Sam's disappointment she was followed not by Lucie, but by the guard and a waiting-gentlewoman. Sam and Robert each removed their hats and made the sort of bow Mr Phillips had long ago taught them to perform: low, unhurried, showing obeisance before a well-born lady, but not sycophancy.

Lady Rich's curtsy was very small, not much more than a nod, but she smiled warmly. "Sir Henry Daines, I believe? You are welcome, sir. And Mr Mountbray also. Please, make yourselves comfortable. My woman will bring refreshments."

The waiting-woman left the room. Sam hoped that if the refreshments included ale or wine, Robert would control both the measure he took and the words he said. He himself felt light-headed enough without the intervention of alcohol. But he knew he must not be complacent. The smallest wrong word or gesture might give the impostors away.

"Now, I believe you have a letter from my Lord Cheetham," said Lady Rich. "May I see it?"

The testing moment had arrived. Sam gathered his courage, and spoke. "Your ladyship, I am obliged to tell you that it is addressed to his daughter, Lady Lucie," he said, striving to sound both deferential and firm. "Lord Cheetham instructed me and my cousin in the most adamant terms to place the letter in her hands, and her hands only."

During the long pause that followed, the sharp expression of Lady Rich's eyes grew even sharper, and a slight frown appeared between her brows. She sat up straighter in her chair, as if she had been alerted to something. She looked carefully at Sam, then at Robert, then at Sam again. Sam wondered if she could see the movement of his heart beneath his doublet and shirt, or hear his uneven breathing. To his left Robert swung his foot nervously – did real gentlemen do that in the presence of ladies? – and to his right the guard's hand lay upon the hilt of his sword.

Then Lady Rich's expression changed. A knowing look crept over her face, and she leaned towards Sam. "I dare say you have heard, during her long absence from home, that Lady Lucie is grown very beautiful?" she said pleasantly.

Fear gripped Sam's throat. That he had been discovered was quite certain. "I have, madam … as has all the county," he managed to say.

"Then you may look upon her beauty with your own eyes," said Lady Rich. She clapped her hands suddenly, making Robert start, half stand up, blush, and sit down again. Hand-clapping was how apprentices were summoned by their masters.

When Matty entered the room, Sam ducked his head and began to pray. But Matty was made of stout stuff. Betraying no recognition of Sam beyond a pink face, which may have been caused by the warmth of the kitchen anyway, she received Lady Rich's instructions to bring her mistress. Prevented by rheumatism from making the customary curtsy, she nodded, and limped from the room, leaving the door open to admit the waiting-woman bearing a laden tray.

Sam could not settle to the food and drink, though Robert had no such scruples. Sam's stomach was afflicted with an agitation he knew not how to contain. But he produced from his pocket the letter that he and Robert had written in the guise of Lord Cheetham.

The footsteps that Sam had last heard hurrying along an upstairs landing at the Palace of Whitehall sounded outside the door, and before Sam could draw breath Lucie was in the room. He and Robert sprang out of their chairs and bowed.

Without looking at Robert, Lucie approached Sam, her hand held out to be kissed. "Sir Henry Daines!" she exclaimed, her eyes alight. "How pleasant to see you again! And Mr Mountbray too. It must be three years or more since we met, my good sirs." She turned to her aunt. "See what fine stock the north-country can produce! And they could not pass through London without calling upon me! How gallant and courteous!"

"Indeed," agreed Lady Rich, indicating for Lucie to sit down so that the visitors, one of whom still held a piece of pastry in his hand, could do so too. "And Sir Henry has a letter…" her light-coloured eyes, full of amusement, rested upon Sam's face for the smallest moment, "from your father, I believe."

Sam gazed and gazed at Lucie. She had never looked so alive. All her senses were attuned to the things she relished – boldness, intrigue, love. Relief that she seemed so well swept over Sam, calming his heart and stomach. Although he went on looking at Lucie while she read the forged letter, he was aware that Lady Rich, engaged in superficial conversation with Robert, was also watching her niece.

"Have you addresses to make to Lady Lucie, Sir Henry?" she asked, looking at Sam sideways. "The compliments you paid her before she entered the room suggest you have."

Lady Rich was no fool, as Sam himself had told Robert. He was sure she had divined the real identities of Sir Henry and his cousin, yet she had not instructed the guard to eject them from the house. Unaccountably, she seemed to be encouraging his suit as graciously as if he really *were* a titled suitor from the north-country.

"You are very kind, my lady," he said, unable to prevent the colour rising to his cheeks. "My primary hope in paying this unexpected call upon your niece is, I confess, that I may be permitted to pay my addresses to her. Encouraged by my good friend Cyril here, I made application to her father, who writes his approval in the very letter Lady Lucie now reads."

"Then I see why you wished to deliver it exclusively into her own hands!" exclaimed Lady Rich. "And I must add my approval to Lord Cheetham's. As her guardian, I give you permission to exchange correspondence with my niece when you return to the north-country."

"I thank you, your ladyship," said Sam, bowing, "with all my heart."

When he raised his head he saw Lucie and her aunt

break the gaze they had held upon each other's faces. Each looked away, and as Lucie turned her face towards him he plainly discerned that her eyes were full of tears.

"And now, gentlemen, the hour is late," said Lady Rich, rising briskly and signalling for the waiting-woman to come forth. "We have, I think, completed our business." She held out her hand to Sam and Robert in turn. "Lady Lucie and I will bid you good night."

Lucie's face was wet with tears. Sam knew, without any possibility of doubt, that her aunt would not ask the reason for this display of emotion. Gratitude overwhelmed him as he bowed again to Lady Rich. "I thank you for seeing my cousin and myself this evening, my lady," he said. "Good night to you. And to you, Lady Lucie."

Lucie could not speak, but even in confusion she retained the daring yet tender quality Sam loved so dearly. He looked at her boldly before he made his bow.

"Good night to you, Sir Henry," said Lady Rich, inclining her head. "And please, do call again when you are next in London. My niece will be pleased to receive you."

In Sam's most far-fetched dreams of the outcome of this evening's escapade, he had not imagined that he would be invited again to the house. He was not a real gentleman; his time was regulated not by his own will, but by that of his masters. And would the costume baskets yield enough clothes to continue the performance?

"I thank you, your ladyship," was his awkward reply, "though I know not when that might be." He turned to Robert. "Come, Cyril, we have presumed too long upon Lady Rich's hospitality. Let us to our lodging."

As soon as the manservant had closed the door behind them, Sam and Robert broke into a run. They ran down the Strand and along Fleet Street, their footsteps loud in the silence, until both were breathless. His chest ready to burst, Sam sat down on a doorstep.

"Do you think she knew?" he asked Robert, who was leaning against the doorpost, exhausted.

"Of course she knew." It was too dark to see Robert's grin, but Sam could hear it in his voice. "She is the cleverest woman in England – save Her Majesty, naturally – and when she has left off being Lord Mountjoy's mistress, I hope she will be mine!"

The Warning

Sam daily thanked God for Lady Rich's wisdom and liberality. The freedom not only to write to Lucie, but to deliver the letters in person without fear of reprisals, was intoxicating. Trust in the truth, Clarice had said, as if she had somehow known that Lady Rich would penetrate deception, convention and even lawbreaking to find it. When other people looked at Sam, they saw an ordinary boy, a player. When Lady Rich had looked at him, dressed illegally in clothes reserved for the rich, she had understood that here was a man who would love and care for her niece better than any genuinely aristocratic suitor.

He was even able, when circumstances allowed, to pretend that Sir Henry Daines had ridden from Northumberland to call at Essex House. Lady Rich would discreetly quit the room, leaving Sam and Lucie to speak in private. On one of these occasions they had gone into the garden, cloaked and hatted against a breezy October day. Lucie sat on a stone seat under a bower of late-flowering roses. A portrait, thought Sam, always a portrait.

"May I ask you something, Lucie?"

"Of course, providing it is not too difficult," she said, mock-demurely.

Sam sat beside her, but did not take her hand in case Lord Essex should be watching from a window. He had been ill recently, and was often in the house. Sam lived in daily fear that Lucie's uncle, who had seen him close up many, many times more than either of her aunts, would recognize him. Lady Rich's ability to charm, persuade and recruit men to her point of view was powerful, but Sam was dubious whether it would work on her brother. "It is a difficult question. But please answer if you can."

Lucie looked concerned. "What is it?"

Sam pondered for a moment before he spoke. "Once, a long time ago, when you and I had not yet even seen each other, Mr Shakespeare held a meeting of the Lord Chamberlain's Men in Mistress Turville's tavern. He wished to discuss how we were to destroy the old theatre we leased from Mr Allen, and build our new one, the Globe. I remember he stood up and said, 'Gentlemen, I stand before you as a poor player, simple and ignorant.'"

Lucie looked doubting, but did not speak.

"He is not simple and ignorant, any more than you or I are, of course," went on Sam. "Neither is he a poor player. But I…" He looked at her fervently. "I *am* a poor player, Lucie. I have nothing but my salary, which depends upon the success or failure of the company, and could cease at any moment. I have no property, no connections, no education beyond what my father and Mr Phillips and my own wits have given me. I have no prospects except those of a skilled man. I must go through my life hoping to sell those skills, just as if I were a bookbinder or a silversmith, to anyone who will pay me for them."

He stopped, unsure how to go on. He had not even broached the question he had begged Lucie to answer. His nerve was faltering.

"Are you telling me you are a poor prospect as a husband?" asked Lucie. "I cannot imagine why, since I know this already. If you are trying to say something else, say it. And where is the difficult question?"

"Oh, Lucie." Sam's apprehension began to disperse. He felt like smiling, though he did not, in case it belied the seriousness of his words. "How often I fall into the trap of thinking you are like other people! But you are not."

She smiled delightedly, and turned a little pink. "The question, if you please, Sir Henry."

"Very well, the question." Her face was serious again. Sam took courage. "If I had not been a player, would you ever have fallen in love with me?" She tried to speak, but he suppressed her. "And if I ceased to be a player, would you cease to love me?"

"That is two questions."

"They are related," said Sam. His heart had begun to thud. "Please, Lucie, tell me the truth."

To his surprise her flush deepened. She turned her head uneasily, hiding her face under the brim of her hat. "Before I answer, will you allow me to ask *you* a question?"

The thudding of Sam's heart had not subsided. The answer he hoped for remained unvoiced. "Of course," he said uncertainly.

"Do you remember what we swore to each other that day in your lodgings? We promised never to betray each other. And then you said that one day I would be yours. You said that, Sam, and I believed it."

"Do you not believe it now?"

There was a long pause, during which Lucie's face remained hidden. A numbing coldness trickled over Sam's body. Was she about to tell him that, enamoured as she was by the life he led, she could not accommodate herself to the role of a player's wife? At last, Sam felt a small hand curl its fingers around the corner of the fur-edged cloak he wore. He looked down at it, speechless with anticipation.

"This is my answer," said Lucie. "As I said that day, I will never betray you for anyone else. I will be faithful to you all my life." Her voice was small, but warm, and although she did not look at him, her hand crumpled the corner of his cloak as if she were reassuring herself of his presence. "It is true that I love you for your acting ability, but that is because of the freedom and joy it gives you. It is not *all* I love you for." She looked at him then, earnestly, with greater conviction in her eyes than he had ever seen before. "Whatever happens, Sam, the freedom and joy will remain, because they are *you*."

He could not embrace her; he certainly could not kiss her, here in the garden. But he took her hand and lifted it to his lips, as Sir Henry Daines would do. "Then you are mine, player or not."

"I have always been yours," said Lucie.

* * *

The Lord Chamberlain's Men had assembled at the Globe for a rehearsal of *Much Ado About Nothing*. Rain fell ceaselessly, so heavily that the raindrops danced furiously on the yard, turning its surface into a lake. Sam dashed across it with William and Robert through light dimmed by December's short days and the glowering sky.

"Why must we rehearse in such inclement weather?" grumbled Mr Pope.

"Because we are commanded by Her Majesty to play at court," announced Mr Shakespeare, "at each of Her Majesty's Christmas celebrations. She is entertaining lavishly this year, at the palaces of Whitehall, Richmond and Nonsuch. We have only a week in which to prepare three plays." He surveyed the company until his eyes rested upon Robert. "We are to be paid handsomely for our pains, and your advancement will come, Master Goughe, once the Master of the Revels's restriction is lifted, and we have our liberty."

"Thank you, sir," said Robert. He did not smile, though. No one did.

"But *when* shall we have our liberty?" asked William. His fair face, less boyish now, Sam thought, with the flares at the side of the stage throwing its bones and shadows into relief, was serious. As William's star continued to rise in the acting profession, the future of the company was increasingly his foremost concern.

The senior men exchanged glances, and after a pause Mr Burbage spoke.

"A lady known to us all expects a child," he stated

decisively. Sam knew he spoke of Lady Essex. "If I were her husband – and I am sure I speak for every man here assembled – I would not risk the well-being of that newborn, or my other children, by behaviour that may be construed as..." he considered his next word carefully, "inadvisable. Let us hope that with this new life comes new wisdom, and that by the time the child's mother is in church again all will be well."

"May the Lord have mercy upon the child's soul," said Mr Pope softly.

"Amen," agreed Mr Shakespeare. "Now, let us to work."

Sam was playing Hero again. He did not mind. Two Christmases ago, when *Much Ado About Nothing* had been performed at the Palace of Whitehall and a beautiful girl had come to the door of the supper room looking for her uncle, Sam had been a resentful apprentice. Now, at the age of eighteen, he was a hired man who knew his value to the company and had left resentment behind. He was not now quite so "short" as the script demanded, but his hair was as "brown" as ever. And anyway, William's portrayal of Beatrice was well loved by the courtly audience. Sam had stopped being envious of William's popularity. He had proved his own ability to impress the crowd.

Mr Burbage had expressed concern for Lord Essex's wife and children, but Lucie's position was equally precarious. Lord Essex had been very unwell, confined to his bed and suffering greatly for many weeks. Recently he had recovered sufficiently to be seen again in society, surrounded as usual by the very men he should have shunned. They were all still banned from court, but they never missed an opportunity to show their refusal to accept their punishment, and their absolute determination not to reform. The whole of London was aware that if illness did not finish off Lord Essex, his recklessness might well do so.

Lucie's letters made increasingly uneasy reading. That morning she had reported that Lord Essex and Lady Rich were to spend the Christmastide with Lord Mountjoy and other friends at Lord Southampton's country house. Lady Essex would be delivered of her third child during their absence, and had begged Lucie to stay with her. *So, dearest,* Lucie had concluded, *I cannot come to court this Christmas, or at any time in the foreseeable future.*

If only the future really *were* foreseeable! Sam had read the letter again, the hairs on the back of his neck standing up as he thought about the house party at Lord Southampton's, and what would be discussed there. Lucie's words were not elaborate or passionate, nor were they charged with any obvious distress. But Sam suspected that the final reckoning of Lord Essex's fate was near.

It was a busy Christmas season. The company took three different plays, all comedies, to the palaces at Whitehall and Richmond, and to Nonsuch, the house that had witnessed Lord Essex's fateful encounter with the half-dressed queen more than a year previously. Her Majesty ignored the absence of Lord Essex and his circle, who were still under banishment from her presence. She seemed at pains to charm and accommodate as never before. After all these years of her reign, though, no one was fooled. Sir Robert Cecil's glittering eyes missed nothing. Today the queen might be giggling like a girl, but tomorrow she would once more become the ruthless empress her subjects knew her to be.

Performing *Much Ado About Nothing* at the Palace of Whitehall affected Sam profoundly. As he spoke Hero's only line in the first scene, he thought how strange it was that a *real* slender, dark-haired girl had changed his life far more than the imaginary one he was playing ever could. Hero remained the same however many times the play was performed, and so did her lover, Claudio. But who could fathom the depths of the transformation Lucie's love had wrought in Sam, and his in her?

He remembered that in *Twelfth Night* someone said, "'If this were played upon a stage now, I could condemn it as an improbable fiction.'" The line always raised an enormous laugh. Sam could not help thinking that despite Mr Shakespeare's wonderful ability to look into the human heart, Sam's own true story of the last two years would still sound to his ears like a far more improbable fiction than any scene in *Twelfth Night*.

Its conclusion was still unwritten, of course. The trial of Lord Essex and his return to Essex House seemed a long way in the past. During these last few months Sam had woken each morning and fallen asleep each night with the same thought. His future lay with Lucie – he was no longer in any doubt of that – but if it proved necessary, could he truly abandon the Lord

Chamberlain's Men, whose approval he had worked so hard to gain?

One January morning Matty, who now used a walking stick, appeared at the door of Mistress Corrie's house. Her face, shadowed already by constant pain, crumpled as she handed him a letter, and she began to cry. "Oh, Master Sam, forgive me, but … oh, I know not what to say!"

Sam helped her into Mistress Corrie's parlour. "No, I won't sit, master," she said when he offered her a seat. "It is better for my poor leg if I stand."

"Matty, what is amiss?" he asked.

She nodded towards the letter in Sam's hand. "That may be the last letter my mistress can write for a long time. And do not come to Essex House any more." Her voice cracked, though her tears were drying. "You will see why when you read my lady's letter. And my leg is so bad now, I do not know if I can come up here again anyway. My lady tells me you will be moving to Southwark, which is too far away."

"Not to Southwark," Sam reassured her hurriedly, though he had not yet settled on an area in which to take new lodgings. "But wherever I live I can meet you near Essex House, Matty, to save your leg." He looked at the woman's stricken face, and added, "If there is any occasion to do so, of course."

"I will leave you to read your letter," said Matty, moving towards the door. "Do not reply."

"Why not?" asked Sam in dismay.

Matty nodded again towards the neatly folded, sealed paper. "You will see."

When she had gone Sam took the letter up to his room. After the afternoon's performance Robert and Nathan had gone to Mistress Turville's, and for all Sam knew, so had William. But carousing in a tavern had lately lost its attraction for Sam himself, and he had come straight home. He sat on his bed and broke the seal on Lucie's letter.

Essex House, 10 January 1601

Dear Sam,

You will be as relieved as I am that my Lady Essex has been delivered of a healthy girl, who has been baptized Dorothy. My aunt is well, but does little save sit in the window with her sewing on her lap. I know not for whom, or what, she is watching. Meanwhile the house is full of undesirable people at all hours, whose disrespectful behaviour causes my Lady Essex great pain. But my Lady Rich has shown me great compassion, and allows me to speak of you to her, in private of course.

Lucie's handwriting now took on an untidy aspect, as if she had hurried to place the words upon the paper. Anxiously, Sam read on.

Oh, Sam! Since I wrote these words Lady Rich has brought distressing news. My Lord Southampton has been set upon in the street by a group of men. He was not robbed, but has been injured – my Lady Rich says stabbed! But do not fear, she is certain he will live. The men shouted something about a warning, and flung at his lordship the most foul oaths. This "warning" must be connected to Lord Essex's recent fall

from the queen's favour. My uncle now fears for his own life.
We are shut in and cannot leave the house. I pray that Matty
is able to take this to you, but I know not when you will next
hear from me. Do not give Matty a reply; Lord Essex is
desperate about spies, and is having all the servants searched.

   Bless you, my dearest love, and may the Lord keep you safe.
   Lucie

Sam walked round and round the room in agitation.
He could not hold this news in his hand without hastening to tell Mr Shakespeare of it. If someone could
attack Lord Southampton so viciously, who would
deny that his lordship's friends – including the senior
members of the Lord Chamberlain's Men – must also
be in danger?

The hour was not late; the river was still busy. Sam
hastened to the ferry. He looked at the dark water
swirling around the ferryman's oar blades, pondering
on how often in the past two years darkness, real and
imagined, had touched him. He tucked his cold fingers
beneath his cloak, where they strayed to the letter
hidden in the breast of his doublet. If Mr Shakespeare
demanded proof of the truth of Sam's report, he would
have to show it to him.

There were low, flickering lights in the windows of
Mr Shakespeare's house. Sam was reminded of another
night when, with equally freezing fingers, he had stood
at Mr Heminges's lighted window and begged his
assistance. That request had been occasioned by Robert's
encounter with violence; Sam's present pilgrimage in the
dark was caused by Lord Southampton's.

He pounded on the door. "Mr Shakespeare, sir! 'Tis Sam Gilburne, sir!"

"Sam? Peace, boy, for God's love!" came Mr Shakespeare's voice. Sam heard bolts being shot and keys turned, and then Sam half stepped, half fell into the room that had seen so many readings, and so many arguments. In a high-backed chair, with his feet in the hearth, sat William Hughes.

"What are you doing here?" asked Sam.

"I could enquire the same of you," said William, unperturbed.

"I have some news for Mr Shakespeare."

"And is this news for my ears alone," Mr Shakespeare asked, rebolting the door, "or may Mr Hughes hear it?"

"He may hear it, sir. It is about Lord Southampton."

Mr Shakespeare sat down on his usual chair. His attention landed keenly upon Sam's face. "Lord Southampton?"

"Yes, sir," said Sam, feeling important. "He has been attacked by villains in the street. I know not the details, but he received a knife wound."

"A knife wound! Good God, not a fatal one!" Mr Shakespeare had half risen to his feet, his eyes luminous in the firelight. He caught hold of Sam's arm. "Speak, boy!"

"I do not believe his life to be in danger," said Sam.

William stood up, the firelight silhouetting his neatly clad frame and lengthening hair. It occurred to Sam that he looked less like a player and more like an idle gentleman with every day that passed. The look he cast Sam plainly said, "Lord Southampton's life may not be in danger from any knife wound, but that is only one way to die!"

Mr Shakespeare rose, releasing Sam's arm, and sat down at his writing desk. "Lady Lucie Cheetham, my Lord Essex's esteemed niece, has a hand in this news, does she not? Let me see the letter."

Sam hesitated, but Mr Shakespeare dismissed his reluctance with a wave of his hand. "Have no fear, boy. As you have seen this past year, I can keep her in my own heart as well as your friend William here ever kept her in his. She is a lovely creature, I must say. But to the business in hand. Give me the letter."

Mr Shakespeare's face remained impassive while he read Lucie's letter. When he had finished he drew a sheet of paper towards him. "Is she your mistress?" he asked Sam amiably as he began to write.

Sam tried not to betray his surprise. "Mistress, sir?"

"That was my word. Have you made defeat of her honour?"

Sam stared. William, laughing, kicked him lightly on the ankle. "He means, have you tumbled her, Sam."

Sam pushed the heel of his hand into the middle of William's chest as hard as he could. William yelped, staggered, and almost fell into the fire.

"Tumbled, is it?" asked Sam sharply. "As if she were a peasant's daughter, ready to raise her petticoats for anyone?"

His heart felt as if it were flying and diving at the same time. He approached the writing table. "Mr Shakespeare, sir," he said emphatically, "Lucie is a lady and I will not hear her virtue discussed between men with whom her acquaintance is slight. Rebuke me if you will, but I must speak my mind as you have yours."

Mr Shakespeare, writing the while, smiled. "Lawyer, lawyer, lawyer," he said. "You have not, then."

Red-cheeked, his heart still racing, Sam turned from him and resumed his place before the hearth. He did not look at William.

"This is a letter to Lady Essex," announced Mr Shakespeare, "congratulating her upon the birth of her daughter, among other compliments. I will walk boldly to the door of Essex House and present it to Lady Essex's servant myself." He turned a tranquil gaze upon Sam. "If Lord Essex insists upon inspecting the contents of the letter, then that is a matter to be resolved between himself and his wife. But I have surreptitiously let her know that her predicament, and that of the other ladies of the house, has not passed unnoticed. While the stout-hearted Robert Goughe, William not-as-brainless-as-he-looks Hughes and I myself live, we will remember them. I hope Lady Essex will tell her niece of the contents of this letter, and that it will warm Lady Lucie's heart."

"Thank you, sir," said Sam humbly.

"Time enough to thank me when they are free. Now, I will away to the ferry. William, do not let the fire go out. We shall all have toasted cheese when I return."

Sam felt exhausted. *Twelfth Night* was to be performed the following afternoon, which was the first Saturday for some weeks upon which the Lord Chamberlain's Men had been granted leave to perform. Sam had been told only yesterday that he was to play Viola, the leading lady. When he had questioned Mr Burbage as to why William, who usually took this part, was playing the leading man instead, Mr Burbage had murmured, "Physical beauty, Sam, physical beauty."

Sam knew this was a joke. A leading man was not supposed to be more beautiful than his leading lady. The real reason, Sam suspected, was that now William's twentieth birthday had passed he was becoming too mature to play girls. Some time in the coming year the role of Beatrice in *Much Ado About Nothing* would be given to Robert or himself. He may even end up playing Titania, William's favourite part, in the ever-popular *Dream*.

For now, though, Sam had not the time to speculate on the coming year. He had a day and a half to learn the lines for Viola and rehearse her moves. He took the script up to the second gallery of the empty theatre and set to memorizing.

But he could not concentrate. Fatigue threatened to overwhelm him. Sleep had been elusive during the weeks since the attack on Lord Southampton. It had turned out that the culprits were Lord Grey de Wilton – a supporter of Sir Robert Cecil – and some of his servants. One of these men's knives had penetrated the earl's clothing, but fortunately had only scratched his flesh.

Lord Grey and his henchmen had been imprisoned, but the effect of the incident upon Lord Essex amounted almost to hysteria. Sam could imagine Lucie's distress as her uncle paced the rooms of Essex House, bemoaning his fate, inventing grievances, making plans as rashly as ever, and surrounding himself with those whose allegiance fed his rebellious fever. Every member of the Lord Chamberlain's Men knew that Lord Essex was putting about the notion that there was a plot afoot to murder him, and whipping up support for this belief. But each man kept his counsel.

"Sam, you are wasting your time."

Robert and William stood before him. The scar on Robert's chin showed very red. Sam realized with concern that it was because his face was very, very white. William's complexion was its usual colour, but in his eyes Sam saw fear. "In God's name, what has happened?" he asked.

Robert took *Twelfth Night* from Sam's hand. "We are not playing this tomorrow afternoon. We are playing *King Richard the Second*."

Sam did not understand. He was about to say so when William spoke in his gravest, most statesmanlike voice. His Mark Antony voice. "Sam, new playbills are already being written. *King Richard the Second* is a command performance."

Command performances were the queen's prerogative. But it was impossible that she would have requested this particular play. "You mean Her Majesty…" Sam began, his brain working furiously.

William silenced him with a piercing look. "It is not Her Majesty's command that we are compelled to obey, but that of Sir Charles Percy and some other members of Lord Essex's circle. They visited Mr Shakespeare at home early this morning and commanded – or *demanded*, more like – that we give *King Richard the Second* tomorrow."

Sam's limbs suddenly felt as if they were made of stuffed sacking, like the scarecrows in his father's fields. Disbelief, swiftly followed by dread, swept over him. He could not move.

Lord Essex's command was that the Lord Chamberlain's Men perform a play about the deposing and murder of a monarch. Not a distant Roman emperor, as in *Julius Caesar*, though that was risky enough, but the regicide committed by English rebels a mere two hundred years ago. Sam's long-held mistrust of *King Richard the Second* seemed well placed.

"This cannot be right, William," he said. "Why would Mr Shakespeare agree to such a thing? Is he not aware of the message Lord Essex wishes to convey to Sir Robert Cecil and the queen by the performance of this play?"

"Of *course* he is," said Robert, shaking Sam's arm in his agitation. "Of *course* he would not have agreed had he been given free choice. They must have threatened him." He shook Sam's arm harder. "These men are dangerous, and becoming more so with each day that passes. Mr Shakespeare could not risk a refusal."

William stood by the rail at the front of the gallery, from where every entrance to the theatre was visible. His eyes worked, darting this way and that, missing nothing that might happen below. Sam wondered, not for the first time, if there would ever come a day when he and his friends could speak freely again.

"Mr Burbage has called a walk-through of *King Richard the Second* for tomorrow morning," Robert informed Sam. "Parts and places as before, he says. Oh, and we are to be paid more than usual. Lord Essex's men gave Mr Shakespeare forty shillings to help 'persuade' him, and he wishes to share it with us all."

Enter Hero

Mr Armin, in whose nature superstition had no foothold, was playing Exton the king killer. Mr Burbage played, as usual, the king about to be killed. Both of them had strong, well-trained stage voices. But neither Sam nor anyone else packed into the Globe that February afternoon heard a word of the death scene.

The noise from the crowd was not like the chorus of approval that accompanied the stabbing of Caesar, or the patriotic cheering with which King Henry the Fifth's speech to his troops was always received. It began slowly, like the murmur of a softly struck drum, in the lower gallery, where Lord Essex's supporters – though not Lord Essex himself or his sister, Lady Rich, who were absent – sat. It rose, becoming louder and spreading wider, until every occupant of all three tiers of the gallery was applauding, hissing, booing, stamping their feet and beating their fists on the rails. Before long the groundlings, many of whom must have been mystified, decided they might as well join in.

It occurred to Sam that the noise was unnerving because it was unidentifiable. It was both approval and disapproval. It was the uninhibited bellowing of a mob, secure in the knowledge that each individual voice would be disguised by the others. It was the response of people who, for the last two hours, had watched the play in a tense atmosphere which they were now relieved to shatter. It was all these things, and yet it was greater than the sum of its parts. It was the sound of unknowable violence.

Backstage, Sam listened. The play was almost over. His work as the Duchess of Gloucester and various minor characters was done, his costumes already folded in the basket, his make-up removed. He had resolved that as soon as ever he could be released, he would run away from this place. But as the noise mounted, and armed servants of the queen began to push their way through the crowd, Sam abandoned all thought of waiting for Mr Shakespeare to dismiss him.

He darted down the steps behind the stage and hurried towards the back door. Halfway there he stopped, turned and entered the storeroom under the stage. Groping in the dark, stumbling over boxes and furniture, cursing and sweating, he flipped open the lid of what he prayed was the correct basket. Fortune was on his side. Sam seized the Juliet cloak, rolled it into a tight bundle, and fled.

Outside the theatre it was an ordinary Saturday afternoon. Dusk would fall soon, and the grey-white sky held the promise of February drizzle. Sam tried to calm himself as he hurried through the Southwark alleyways. Feeling in his pocket for his share of the forty shillings, he hailed the first boatman he saw. "If you please, master, the Strand!"

He splashed into the shallows and made a leap for the boat. As the oarsman pulled away, Sam fixed his eyes upon the north bank of the river, calculating. He could get to his destination in a quarter of an hour. The play would have ended by now, but as the Globe was filled to capacity it would be over half an hour before the last member of the audience could get out. The ferries and boatmen would be very busy; Lord Essex's men would have to wait. By Sam's reckoning, an hour would pass before they returned to Essex House.

The boatman seemed to catch Sam's mood of urgency. Although rowing against the current, he quickly reached the mooring below the Strand. Sam jumped out before the boat berthed, hardly noticing his soaking feet. Living with Nathan Field had taught Sam some lessons in remaining unobtrusive. He stowed the Juliet cloak under his own, pulled down his hat, dipped his head and set off towards Essex House, keeping close to the high walls of the other houses.

St Clement Danes tolled five o'clock as he stole up the alleyway and opened the side gate. He tried the side door without much hope. It was locked and, he suspected, barricaded. Sam cursed silently. In making it difficult for their enemies to enter, the occupants of the house had confounded their friends too.

He stepped gingerly round the wall to the back of the house, where the windows of the main room gave on to the garden, which sloped to the river. The room was in darkness, with curtains drawn. But Sam could hear raised voices from somewhere within the house. Their words were indistinct, but he guessed that the argument was between Lord Essex and Lady Rich.

They were in an upstairs room. Sam stepped back and looked up at the window, which was closed. It was evident that Lord Essex was troubled, and Lady Rich distraught. She was sobbing, with the screaming sobs of deep distress. Lord Essex paced the floor. Again and again as he came near the window Sam heard his voice, sometimes a bellow, sometimes a screech, or a whine, or an impatient shout. Sam could not see his face, as the room was almost dark, but he could imagine it.

The queen now knew that Essex House was the breeding ground of the rebellion she had long suspected, and of which she had been given a barely disguised warning in the form of *King Richard the Second*. By now she would have tripled the guards around the Palace of Whitehall. Lord Essex's hatred of Sir Robert Cecil had turned him irrevocably against the ruler he had served loyally for his entire life, and whose friendship he had long basked in. Now, Sam realized as he cowered in the twilit garden, Lord Essex's long-awaited hour of action was upon him.

But Lord Essex did not know what to do. Should he raise the rebellion, regardless of its outcome? Or should he repent, kiss the hem of the queen's gown and beg her forgiveness? Was it worth risking the large probability of disaster for the small possibility of glory? Either way, events had gone too far. His death warrant, and those of his associates, might as well be already signed.

That was why Lady Rich was crying. She knew that whatever her brother decided to do, her head was in danger too. As the earl's sister and a known member of his circle, she had been banned from court along with all the others. And the queen did not scruple to punish women. Her own half-sister, Queen Mary, had perished at her hand.

This thought made Sam feel sick. The queen's spies would keep her informed of Lord Essex's whereabouts. Once he and his supporters were all in Essex House she would send armed men along the Strand. They would break down the barricaded doors and attack the occupants of the house. There would be casualties. The innocent would suffer as well as the guilty.

Sam's queasiness turned to resolve. Lord Essex's hour may be upon him, but so was Sam's. He must find Lucie before her uncle's followers returned from the play.

It was darker now. Sam left his hiding-place in the garden and felt his way back to the side door. He tried to remember what he had seen behind it when Lucie had met him there. Doors opening off a hallway. Doors that must lead to rooms. In that part of the house they would be storerooms, pantries, sculleries.

Sam knew that a pantry must have ventilation or the food would spoil. The farmhouse pantry at home had a square hole in the wall covered by loosely woven muslin, to keep out flies but let in air. Surely the Essex House pantry must be somewhere near? He must act quickly, because when the play-goers returned they would demand food, and the servants would set to work.

He began to search for the pantry window. His

fingers groped over brick and stone and ivy, and window frames and glass and metal. Then, as the church bell sounded the quarter hour, his hand encountered the familiar texture of stretched muslin. The hole it covered was rectangular, and very small. Too small for a man, certainly, but not, Sam fervently hoped, for "short" Hero.

Even allowing for his growth of the last two years, he was still slighter and lighter than anyone in the company except Nathan. The thought of Nathan's incredulity when – if – Sam related this evening's adventure spurred him on. He tore away the muslin, threw the Juliet cloak and his own outer clothing through the hole, then hoisted himself head first after them. Gritting his teeth, he eased his body through.

The smell of cheese told him that this was the dairy pantry. He knew from his days living at Mr Phillips's house that pantries where liquor was stored were always locked. Praying that at Essex House cheese, milk and butter were not considered worth stealing, he dressed himself, found his way to the door and lifted the latch. The hinges worked silently, and Sam found himself in the flagstoned corridor. It led to a hall, from where a dogleg staircase rose to a gallery. Silent in his soft-soled boots, Sam took the stairs three at a time.

There was no light in the gallery beyond that which spilled from the hall below. Sam slipped between two large storage cabinets and listened. Lord Essex and his sister were still behind one of these doors, though Sam could now only hear a masculine voice. Suddenly, Lady Rich opened the door. Sam held his breath, thanking

Providence for the thrifty housekeeping that kept the gallery so dark.

"I shall go to my Lady Essex, now, my lord," she told her brother. "She and Lady Lucie must be wondering what is happening."

"Then let them wonder," came Lord Essex's angry voice from inside the room. "Since I know not what is happening, why should they?"

"Their fate is in your hands, Robert," said Lady Rich gravely.

"Their fate be damned! Leave me."

She hesitated. "Robert—"

"Get out of my sight!"

He must have thrown something – a goblet, perhaps – because Lady Rich flinched, and Sam heard a crash. As she turned her face caught the light from below. That she had long been weeping was all too evident. With a sinking heart Sam observed to himself that this courageous woman, who had done so much for him and Lucie, would weep a great deal more yet. She picked up her skirts and hurried along the gallery to another door, upon which she knocked softly. It was opened by Lady Essex, without her cap and with her baby daughter in her arms. "What does he say? Have you persuaded him?" she asked her sister-in-law urgently.

Lady Rich dismissed her questions with a gesture of frustration, and then the door closed behind them. Sam felt helpless. There was about half an hour left before Lord Essex's friends arrived back from *King Richard the Second*. Maybe less, if his luck did not last. They would surely rekindle the fire of rebellion in Lord Essex, that his wife and sister were trying to kill. It would be merely a matter of hours before the confrontation.

He wondered if Lucie were in the room with Lady Essex. She might be silently tending the children, or sitting at her needlework frame. No, she would not be doing either of those things. Sam felt stupid. Did he not know her better, after more than two years? She would not sit passively while the tide of her uncle's insane undertaking, which had lapped round her feet for months, rose and drowned her. She would fight it, and she would expect Sam to do the same. What had she said that day when he had first come here? "I knew you were looking for me, like a knight coming to rescue a damsel." Now, more than a year later, Lucie must again be hoping that he was looking for her. Her courage in staying with Lady Essex when she could be safe in Northumberland was undoubted; he must match her courage with his own.

At any moment he could be discovered by a servant. In times of crisis candles still had to be lit, water brought to chambers, floors swept and tables laid. Crouching in the shadows, Sam was grateful for the years of Mr Phillips's voice training. He could control his breathing, though not his heartbeat. But at last Lady Rich came out of the room, carrying a candle. She walked towards the cupboards between which Sam was hiding. It was too late for him to slip away. He flattened himself against the wall, trusting the darkness would cover him.

But Lady Rich was a courtier, accustomed to spies and dissemblers of all kinds. Even in distress she was alert. When she came alongside Sam, she stopped. A look of consternation, then of astonishment, showed on her face. "Master Gilburne!" she gasped. She put her hand over her mouth. Her eyes were very bright. "What are you doing here? Only a deranged person would enter this house tonight!"

Sam kept his nerve. She had helped him before; she might help him again. "Where is Lucie?" he whispered. "I must get her away from here."

"Indeed you must, if you love her."

"I do love her."

Tears came again to her eyes. She looked earnestly into Sam's face. "At the end of the gallery is a room with an arched door. Open it and you will find your Lucie. Waste no time; flee." She raised the candle. Her eyes were filled with sadness. "I will never see you again, Sam Gilburne. God speed."

"If I could take you and Lady Essex, and the children—"

She put up her palm. "Think not of us. I cannot be other than my brother's sister, and am under suspicion myself. The queen will have mercy on Lady Essex for her children's sake. But Lucie is wholly innocent, and unprotected except by you. Now go."

Sam obeyed. The room behind the arched door was a closet, with linen stored around the walls. Cold, unlit and uncomfortable though it was, Lucie had chosen it as a hiding-place. When Sam entered she gasped in fright.

"It is I, dearest," he whispered.

Her relief was so overwhelming that she lunged at him, almost knocking him over, and hung about his neck. "I was going to tie the sheets together and lower myself from the window," she told him, beginning to cry. "I was very frightened, but I would have done it!"

"I know you would," soothed Sam, kissing her, stroking her hair, holding her so tightly that her feet came off the floor. She was as light as a child.

"I was waiting for the sound of their boots, Sam." She was sobbing now; the words came out jerkily. "And all the time I hoped … I hoped that—"

"You hoped that I would come, and I have." He set her down. Her legs buckled, but he caught her before she fell. "Lucie, we must go now, we cannot wait even for a minute. Here, I have brought the Juliet cloak. No one will know you once you have this on." He put it round her thin shoulders. "Come now," he coaxed, his heart full of love and sorrow, "we must leave this place."

Along the gallery, down the stairs, over the flagstones to the kitchen door they went. But there they stopped. A piece of wood had been nailed across the side door. Lucie clung to Sam in panic as he pushed her into the pantry and began to remove his cloak and doublet. "We cannot use the front door, so the only way out of the house is the way I came in," he explained. "There is grass below the window on the other side. You will not be hurt."

"Wait," said Lucie, beginning to untie the hooped farthingale she wore under her skirt. Abandoning it among the milk churns, she slipped through the space easily. By the time Sam joined her she had put on the cloak and was waiting by the gate, looking more than ever like Juliet in the Friar's cell, ready to take Romeo's hand in marriage.

Suddenly her body tensed. "Listen!"

Sam pulled her close to the wall. At the Strand end of the alley, Lord Southampton, Lord Mountjoy and Sir Charles Danvers led a straggling band of Lord Essex's supporters back to the house. In contrast to what he had seen earlier that day at the theatre, they seemed subdued. Like their leader, they knew the end – whatever it turned out to be – was near.

Lucie was still sniffing back tears. Sam put his arm round her shoulders and led her towards the river. "Within this half hour, my dearest love," he told her, "you will be safe. Now, cover your head."

She put up the hood. As she and Sam settled down in the boat and the oarsman pulled away, the folds of the cloak lay around her like the robes of a marble statue. The flare in the prow of the boat threw the reflection of river ripples on her face. She looked more beautiful and more sad than Sam could ever have dreamed.

"Thank you for being my knight, Sam Gilburne," she said.

The Surrender

Sam awoke with a violent start. He had been dreaming of drowning, and had been so convinced of imminent death that relief at finding himself safe in bed overpowered him. As the hammering of his heart subsided, he laid his head more comfortably upon the pillow and prepared to go back to sleep.

But then he recollected that he was not on his own narrow mattress. This was a large bed, with curtains all around. There was enough light for him to see the pattern on them; it must be well after sunrise. He sat up. There, on the pillow beside him, was the unmistakable hollow left by another head.

Last night's events flooded back. Lucie had fallen asleep in Mr Shakespeare's bed. Sam had offered to sleep on a straw pallet on the floor of the main room, while Mr Shakespeare put up in the small chamber he used for overnight guests. But Mr Shakespeare had refused.

"Sam, go to your lady," he had insisted. "You are as good as married, and as the hero of the hour, you should have a comfortable rest. God knows what the morrow will bring, but you must be prepared for it."

Sam had lain beside Lucie in the gathering darkness, listening to her regular breathing until fatigue had overwhelmed him. Now, she had woken and risen before him. The silk dress she had worn yesterday, and the Juliet cloak, lay upon a chair. Sam struggled into his clothes and put on his boots. As he descended the stairs he could hear murmured conversation and the clink of silver. They were having breakfast.

"Good morning, Sam!" Mr Shakespeare greeted him as he opened the door. "Have a muffin. I always have muffins for breakfast on Sundays. Did you sleep well?"

"Yes, thank you, sir." Sam sat down next to Lucie. She looked refreshed, but anxious still. Over a plain woollen dress she wore an apron, and her hair was covered by a servant's cap. Sam did not comment on this, but took a muffin. "Thank you, sir," he said again.

"I thought it prudent to ask my housekeeper to disguise Lady Lucie," explained Mr Shakespeare. "In case any unexpected visitors appear."

Lucie put down her porridge spoon and pushed the dish away. Sam, too, had little appetite, but he set to work on his muffin, to please Mr Shakespeare. "Dressed like that, she reminds me of my sister, Clarice," he said. "Though Clarice's apron would be dirtier. My mother is forever scolding her."

"But what are aprons for, if not to get dirty?" asked Lucie. Her eyes softened. She was trying to smile.

"My opinion precisely," said Mr Shakespeare. He looked at Lucie, then at Sam, and gave a small sigh.

"We shall get through this day together," he told them, "whatever it may bring."

"Thank you, sir," said Lucie, dipping her head. "We are very grateful, are we not, Sam?"

Sam nodded. There was a lot to be grateful for. When he and Lucie had alighted from the hired boat at Southwark they had gone straight to William's lodging house. They had knocked repeatedly on the door, but William had not appeared. Sam had concluded that he must be at Mistress Turville's, drinking away uncomfortable memories of the afternoon. But the tavern was in Shoreditch, back on the north side of the river, and anyway he could no more take Lucie to a tavern than leave her to wait alone in a Southwark street.

Lucie had begun to cry again. As Sam had comforted her, the promise Mr Shakespeare had made about Lucie and her aunts had floated into his memory. "While Robert, William and I live, we will remember them."

To Sam's relief, Mr Shakespeare had opened the door before they had reached it. "Come in, come in," he had urged. "I guessed where you had gone at the end of the play, Sam." He had looked quizzically at Lucie. "And that looks like Nathan's cloak from *Romeo and Juliet*."

"We throw ourselves upon your mercy, sir," Lucie had said, lowering the hood.

"Indeed?" Mr Shakespeare had given Sam a companionable look over Lucie's bowed head. "Then I have no choice but to dispense it. Do you like spiced wine?"

Lucie, exhausted, had gone to bed as soon as she had swallowed the warmed wine Mr Shakespeare had insisted she take. Sam had followed not long after. Before he fell asleep he had heard the sounds of bolts and keys, and Mr Shakespeare instructing his housekeeper not to open the door to anyone without his permission. For the time being, Lucie was safe. But what would happen to Lady Essex, Lady Rich and the children?

This question prodded uncomfortably at Sam's peace during the several tense hours that followed breakfast. The silence in Mr Shakespeare's house was broken only by the sound of church bells. Lucie sat on a stool in the corner, pretending to read. Sam, too restless even to pretend, went repeatedly to the window and inspected the street. There were few passers-by, and no callers. But most importantly, there were no armed guards.

Dinner was brought, but little of it was eaten. Lucie did not even approach the table. Three o'clock, then four, five and six o'clock struck. As the cold February darkness descended again, and twenty-four hours had passed since Sam had thrown the Juliet cloak through the pantry window at Essex House, Lucie's nerve gave way.

"I can bear this no longer, sir," she said to Mr Shakespeare, rising from her chair and beginning to untie the apron she still wore. "I must know what has happened. Someone must know. Why has no one come? Am I not to know if my uncle, or any of my relatives, have survived this day?"

Her eyes glittered in the candlelight. Her face was paler than Sam had ever seen it. His heart folded with pity. "Lucie…" he began, taking her by the shoulders.

"Leave me be." She shrugged off his hands. "Mr Shakespeare, unlock the door, if you please. I must find out what has passed since I left Essex House."

Mr Shakespeare also rose. "I cannot do as you ask, my lady," he said steadily. "The danger may not yet be over."

"I am ready to take my chance."

"That I do not doubt. But I beg you, have patience."

"Have patience!" Lucie was incensed. "I have borne the waiting patiently all day, sir, but my heart is too oppressed to bear it all evening too. I will go, I say. Open the door, or I swear—"

Her words were obliterated by the pounding on the door of several fists, and the knocking sound of a pikestaff, or perhaps a sword. Lucie yelped with fear. She caught tight hold of Sam. "It is them! They have come to get me, and take me to prison. Oh, my dearest!"

"It is not, and they have not," announced Mr Shakespeare, who had been peering out of the window. He unbolted the door, turned the lock and opened it to reveal a hot-looking William Hughes, carrying a stout stick, and an equally sweaty, but even more breathless, Robert Goughe. "What news?" he asked them. "Is it all over?"

"It is," gasped William. He collapsed into a chair. "Lord Essex and Lord Southampton have been taken to the Tower, and many others imprisoned elsewhere."

"The Tower!" Lucie leaned heavily against Sam. He helped her to her corner stool, where she sat down slowly, her eyes fixed upon William.

Robert, panting, stood by the door as Mr

Shakespeare locked it again. He took off his cap and hung his head. "Yes, my lady. Sir Christopher Blount is dead, and so is Lord Essex's page, who defended his master to the last."

"Master Tracey!" Lucie's voice broke, and the tears she had kept back all day welled up. "He was younger than I am! Poor boy! What happened, Robert?"

"Sit down, Master Goughe, and tell us what you know," said Mr Shakespeare. "You too, William. Here, take some ale." He brought the pitcher and goblets from the table. "And there is cheese, and cold beef, if you are hungry."

Robert was always, in Sam's experience, hungry. But neither he nor William seemed eager to eat. "Thank you, sir," said William between gulps of ale. "We have run a long way. This is very welcome."

"But now, to your story," urged Mr Shakespeare.

Robert sat down. He looked gaunt, with the remains of shock in his eyes. "Early this morning, Nathan Field, who had been out for hours, came and shouted for me to come out. I ran down with him to Ludgate to see what was happening."

He took a draught of the ale and wiped his lips on his sleeve. "And what did you see?" asked Sam.

"We saw Lord Essex, who looked very wild, striding along towards the Strand, leading his men, shouting, 'For the queen! For the queen! A plot is laid for my life!'" said Robert. "But the crowd were confused. Why did a man saying he was for the queen seem to be raising a rebellion against her? Not one of them joined him."

William took up the story. "That was when I got there. I did not go home last night, but slept at Mr Pope's house, near St Paul's. We noticed people gathering in the street, and went to see what they were looking at. They said that Lord Essex and his men had passed by this morning, going towards the City of London, but had not been able to gather more supporters. Then suddenly we saw Lord Essex marching back again, with very few followers and a face like thunder. Mr Pope and I found Robert and Nathan, but then the guards started to clear away the crowds."

"That was the first moment I knew there would be bloodshed," confessed Robert. "I was frightened, and wanted to go home, and so did Master Pope. But Nathan and William were inclined to stay as long as ever they could, so when Master Pope went, I stayed with them."

"Very brave, Robert," said Mr Shakespeare.

"Thank you, sir."

"What did you do next?" asked Lucie.

"We went to the Three Bells on Ludgate Hill and watched from the upstairs windows," said William. "The queen's men fixed a chain across the road. Lord Essex and his men halted before the chain and the two sides exchanged words. We could not hear what they said, but Lord Essex seemed to be furious, running to and fro like a madman. And then Sir Christopher Blount drew his sword and charged, and was struck down. That was when young Tracey was killed, too. It was all confusion, and we could not see very clearly. But then Lord Essex called to his men to stay their hands."

William turned with sympathy to Lucie. "They all went down to the river to get boats to take them to Essex House, as they could not get there by the street. They were all much shaken by how easily those two lives had been lost, my lady."

Lucie's eyes widened. "So Lord Essex and his men were not arrested and taken away?"

"No." William paused, and exchanged a look with Robert. Something was clearly troubling them both. "The queen's men seemed reluctant to do it," William told Lucie. "If Sir Christopher Blount had not threatened them, I do not believe there would have been any loss of life at that point."

"The queen ever loved Lord Essex," said Lucie into the silence that followed. "She must have ordered her men to give him every chance to retrieve the situation. But he blundered on, to his downfall."

"No one knows exactly what happened then," went on William. "Guards with pikes were threatening anyone that dared set foot upon the roadway. It was only when we saw Lord Essex and Lord Southampton being brought to the Tower that we heard that they had barricaded themselves into Essex House. The rebels had held out against the queen's troops for several hours."

"Oh, my poor aunts!" wailed Lucie. "And the children!"

"Fear not, they are safe," said William. "Lady Rich pleaded with her brother to see reason, and at length Lord Essex surrendered. He opened the door, and he and each of his followers knelt and delivered up their swords to the Lord Admiral, who agreed to let Lady Essex and Lady

Rich and the children remain in the house."

"Thank God!" Lucie prayed briefly. Then she opened her eyes and looked sharply at William and Robert. "Has all this been confirmed?"

"It has, my lady," said Robert. "A notice was posted upon the Tower gate, to appease the crowd that had gathered there. Now all that remains is for the fate of Lord Essex and Lord Southampton to be known."

Lucie sighed. "That is not in doubt, gentlemen."

"Come, do not despair," William urged her. "Her Majesty may yet show clemency towards your uncle."

"Thank you, William," said Lucie gently, "but it is her very love for him which has hastened his fall. He thought he was immune to punishment, and will pay with his life for his presumption."

Mr Shakespeare, who had been silent a long time, rose and began to unbolt the door. "Come, my friends," he said without urgency, "now that all is calm, let us go out and breathe the air."

Sam took Lucie's hand and kissed it, and drew it around his waist. She did not smile, but in her eyes glimmered the sense of deliverance they all felt. Sam put the Juliet cloak around her shoulders, and they followed Mr Shakespeare and the others.

The streets were quiet, even for a Sunday evening. Bells rang for evensong in all the surrounding churches, but few worshippers passed by. The air which Mr Shakespeare had desired to breathe was damp, and full of Southwark's pungent smells. The shape of the Globe rose in the blue-black twilight like a fortress. As they turned their backs to it, and made their way towards the greener spaces that lay beyond the last few straggling houses, Sam's feelings over-powered him.

"Tell me that you love me," he whispered to Lucie.

"I love you," she replied obediently.

"Then may I ask you formally, since I never have, if you will marry me?"

"You may, and I will." Her fingers tightened round his, though she did not look at him. Her eyes were fixed upon Mr Shakespeare's back view as he strolled along, sniffing the air. "My father must be persuaded. And we know in whose hands the accomplishment of that lies."

"Lady Rich will assist," said Sam.

"True, but Mr Shakespeare must vouch for you as a gentleman, or my father will never agree to give me to you."

Sam pondered. He thought about Hero, almost killed by her lover's false accusation. He thought about Duke Orsino and Olivia, tricked into believing a woman was a man. He thought about the two pairs of lovers in *A Midsummer Night's Dream*, driven to despair by mischief and misunderstandings. But all these situations resolved themselves, and the plays ended happily. If Mr Shakespeare's brain could produce all these lovers' obstacles, and all their solutions, then surely he would devise a way to ensure a happy ending for Sam and Lucie?

"Fear not," he told her. "I will speak to him."

But Sam did not need to. Soon after they returned to the house, and William and Robert had gone home,

Mr Shakespeare sat down at his writing desk and took up his pen. "I am writing to Lord Cheetham," he announced. "I expect you can both guess the import of my letter."

Sam and Lucie exchanged looks.

"I have every confidence that when Lord Cheetham hears of Sam's rescue of his daughter he will have no hesitation in giving his consent for your marriage," declared Mr Shakespeare. "I will of course also tell him of Sam's trustworthy record as an apprentice and hired man of the Lord Chamberlain's Men, and of my own approval of the match. I may also suggest that Master Gilburne has the makings of a lawyer, should Lord Cheetham choose to bestow the means upon him of taking up that profession."

Sam fixed his eyes upon Lucie, and she nodded. "Thank you, sir," he said to Mr Shakespeare, "but I do not want to be a lawyer. I am a player, and a player I shall always be."

"And I," added Lucie, "shall be honoured to be a player's wife."

Mr Shakespeare put down his pen, sat back in his chair and regarded them both for a moment. Then he smiled in a way Sam recognized from many a rehearsal. It was the smile of satisfaction. "Good," he said. "If Lady Lucie Cheetham is willing to marry into the acting profession – her father's consent allowing – there is hope that, one day, to be a player will be as desirable an occupation as any other."

"I am indebted to the acting profession," said Lucie, smiling too, "for it has given me Sam."

Mr Shakespeare nodded, and again took up his pen. "Now, I believe the best way to convey this letter to Lord Cheetham's house is for you to carry it there yourselves." He wrote a few words, scrutinized them, then continued. "And since Sam, gentleman though he is in all but family, has little money, I am informing Lord Cheetham that I will pay your passage, and send my manservant as your escort."

"And Matty?" asked Lucie. "Thank you, sir, but I cannot go home without my faithful maid, who took and brought our letters for so long."

Mr Shakespeare looked carefully at Lucie, then at Sam, who tried to look inscrutable. "Very well, my lady," he said, writing some more. "Matty as well." He slid Lucie another look. "Anyone else? No dogs, or cats?"

"No. No, sir, that is all. Thank you," replied Lucie, confused. She was less accustomed than Sam to Mr Shakespeare's style of gentle mockery.

The letter sealed, Mr Shakespeare held it out solemnly to Sam. "You had better be off at first light," he advised, "and obtain a licence from the Guild Hall before you can make your journey."

"What if the Bailiff will not sign a licence for me?"

Mr Shakespeare looked meaningfully from Sam to Lucie and back again. "If he will not sign for you, he will sign for the daughter of Lord Cheetham."

Sam took the letter. He wondered if he were required to make a speech of gratitude, but a glance at Mr Shakespeare's expression told him it would be unnecessary. "Thank you, sir," he said. "I am for ever in your debt."

"No, you are not," said Mr Shakespeare, rising from the desk and picking up the candle-holder. "But you are still in my employ. I expect you back in London in two weeks' time, ready to perform in the play I have at last finished, about the Prince of Denmark." He gave Sam a withering look. "And no, you are not to be the prince himself. That privilege will go to Mr Burbage. You are to be in a petticoat and wimple again, playing the queen of Denmark. How will that suit you, do you think?"

"Very well, sir," said Sam, grinning.

"Then let us to bed," said Mr Shakespeare. "It has been a long and anxious day, and on the morrow you have an early start. I bid you good night."

When Mr Shakespeare had bowed to Lucie and gone, Sam took a candle and prepared to follow him. But Lucie's touch on his arm stopped him. "Sam," she said softly. "I am happy, but I cannot forget my uncle's situation. He is in a dungeon awaiting sentence of death. Please, before we go, I must send a message to my dear aunts."

Sitting at the desk, she took up Mr Shakespeare's pen and dipped it in the inkpot. Sam sat down by the fire and watched her candlelit face as she concentrated on her words. He thought about how William had told him that he and Robert would dance at Sam's wedding. Despite everything, he smiled to himself at the prospect.

"There," said Lucie, folding the letter. "We can

deliver this when we collect Matty tomorrow. How surprised they will all be!"

She rose, and Sam put his arm about her shoulders. In his other hand he held the candle. When it had lighted them up the stairs and into Mr Shakespeare's bedchamber, Sam folded Lucie in his arms, and they clung to each other.

"Mr Shakespeare must approve of you very highly," said Lucie. Sam could feel her eyelashes and her breath on his cheek. "He allows us to sleep in his bedroom together, but trusts that we will not engage in what I believe are called 'country matters' until we are married."

"I know not what Mr Shakespeare thinks," Sam told her softly, "but I am an honourable man, and even under such tempting circumstances, I will never take advantage of a lady."

She stood back, holding her skirt out and turning this way and that. "I am not dressed like a lady today," she said. "Do you think the apron becomes me?"

Sam took her arm and drew her towards him. "No," he said truthfully. "I do not like to see you dressed like my sister. And you no longer have to wear a disguise, Lucie. Take the apron off."

He had never given her a command before. Her expression changed. For a moment he thought he had displeased her, and was about to abase himself – bow, kiss her hand, whatever would appease her. But she stepped even closer to him, her eyes never leaving his face, and slid both her arms round his waist. He could feel her shallow, warm breathing. Into her eyes swam a look he had dreamed about, but never thought to see. He realized with a sword-sharp stab that her desire for him was as great as his for her. His blood was roused; she raised her lips to meet his. As he kissed her he reached behind her back and seized hold of the apron-strings.

"Sam," she whispered, her hands travelling over his body, "I know what you said about taking advantage of a lady, and that is quite right. But do you think, despite being such an honourable man, that you might consider taking advantage of a serving wench?"

—*THE END*—